MW00851199

UNMASKED

---

7 DEADLY SINS: PRIDE

7 DEADLY SINS
BOOK 6

HALEY RHOADES

Haley Rhoades

HR

Haley Rhoades
Author

eBook ISBN: 978-1-959199-58-8
Paperback ISBN: 978-1-959199-28-1

Cover by @Germancreativ on Fiverr

❀ Created with Vellum

DEDICATION

In memory most amazing woman I ever met--
Dawn Holt 7/20/71-2/15/23
I will celebrate the "oopsies" in my life
and live for the "BAHAHA" moments.
You touched so many lives, and you will be greatly missed.

Your positivity, smile, and friendship meant
more to me than I could ever express.
I hope to continue your crusade against colon cancer,
our Remi & Nala books series,
and attempt to spread sunshine and smiles
like you did on a daily basis.

To Enhance Your Reading:
Check out the **Trivia Page** at the end of this book
before reading Chapter #1.
No Spoilers—I promise.
Look at my Pinterest Boards for my inspirations
for characters,
recipes, and settings.
(Link at the end of the book.)

Prefer your romance on the **sweeter** side?
Look for this story under my **PG-13** author name Brooklyn Bailey.
BrooklynBailey.com

PROLOGUE
TAG

I scan through my friends' Instagram feed. Post after post, their photos detail the end-of-spring-semester trip I planned for us. While chilly sixty-degree rain falls outside my window here in Iowa, they enjoy sand, drinks, and bikinis in Key West.

While part of me wishes to be anywhere else but here, the other part of me is glad Mona's suffering ended. If it needs to rain, today is the perfect day. When I stood at the graveside, I imagined the light sprinkles were Mona's tears falling from her new home in heaven. Cancer ravaged her body for two long years this second time; I like that she no longer suffers.

Soft raps on my closed office door interrupt my silent lamentation.

"Enter," I bark, my voice gravelly with emotion.

Bonnie sticks her head in; her puffy eyes and blotchy face tug at my heart.

"A lawyer's here to see you," she informs.

"Please see them in," I instruct.

I leave my stance at the window, returning to the leather chair at my desk, pulling up my lawyer's contact on my cell phone.

"Gentlemen," I greet the two suits entering my office.

I swear Bonnie said a lawyer, yet two sit across from me now. The older of the two wears a gray off-the-rack, pin-striped suit, a cream dress shirt, and red tie. He has dark circles under his eyes and sports a generic haircut. The younger man dresses immaculately in a tailored Tom Ford blue suit, a dress shirt with French cuffs, and Italian leather shoes. I easily assess he cares about his appearance, styles his hair with products, and follows a skin care regime.

"I'm Morty Newman and this is David," the older gentleman informs, extending his hand across the desk.

As I shake his hand, the younger man states, "David Newman."

I wonder why he thinks it necessary to correct his father by sharing his full name? They share a last name; I assume that means it is a family firm.

"It is a pleasure to meet you," I greet, assuming they know my name as they appeared on my doorstep. "I contacted my lawyer; he should be here any minute."

"That was not necessary," Morty scowls.

"Perhaps we should inform you why we are here," David suggests, attempting to be all business.

Perhaps that information should have been shared before they plopped their butts in my office chairs.

"We work for Mona Whately," Morty states.

Works? Works for Mona? She died four days ago; he worked for Mona. We lowered her into the ground hours ago. Why are they here?

Two loud knocks at the door precede Justin's entry. His father follows close behind him, still in their suits from the funeral.

"Mike and Justin Green," I introduce them. "This is Morty and David Newman. Gentlemen, Mike is my attorney."

The men exchange handshakes. Justin and David share a private conversation. It seems they know each other socially.

"I don't mean to keep you," Morty begins. "I am here on behalf of Mona Whatley. While we will meet at a much later date regarding her estate and will, today I am here on a more pressing matter."

I share a pointed stare with Justin. As my much older stepsister, Mona and I rarely found time to visit one another. She fought her battle with breast cancer in Des Moines while I attended college in Iowa City. I am not sure if we were close. While we rarely saw one another, we shared multiple phone calls each week. *I guess that counts.*

"Mona chose you as legal guardian of her fifteen-year-old daughter," he pauses, tilting his head, while making eye contact with me. "As you agreed to take over guardianship, it should come at no surprise that I must process documents prior to leaving Emma in your care."

"What do I do with a 15-year-old girl? I'm not even her blood relative," I spout before I think better of it.

"You are the only family she has," Morty reiterates what I already know.

What? Bile creeps up my throat, and fear courses through my veins. *I am twenty-years-old; I cannot be legal guardian to my step-niece.* A heavy boulder sinks in my stomach, as a phone conversation with Mona over a year ago comes to mind. *She was serious. Shit!* I laughed it off and she did not correct me. She meant it when she stated she wanted me to take care of Emma when her body gave out. I expected Mona to beat it like she did the first time she took chemo.

"Your housekeeper escorted Emma to the kitchen so we can take care of business." Morty speaks as if this is no big deal.

This is a big deal; it is huge. I am a college student and athlete, and he delivers paperwork that makes me guardian of a fifteen-year-old girl. In essence, I will be her father. I shake my head.

"Tag," Mike nudges my shoulder with his forearm.

I glance up at him towering over me from the right of my desk chair.

"The paperwork is in order," Mike informs me. "You need to sign here and here." He points as he speaks.

I take the pen he holds and sign. I am not sure what I am signing. *Emma is a human; am I really signing a paper twice to take over control of her? I barely take care of myself these days, and now I am an adult in charge of a teenage girl.*

"We won't keep you," Morty says, rising from his chair.

David follows his lead. The five of us shake hands, and Justin speaks to the men as he guides them out the office door.

Forearms on my desktop, I hold the stack of papers in my hands. I stare at the black type on the white background, but all I see is a blur.

"Well, that was a surprise," Tag professes, plopping into a chair opposite me. "Why didn't you tell me? How long have you known you would be her guardian?"

Resting the papers on the desk, I find both Mike and Tag staring at me.

I shrug, "Mona spoke to me about it a year ago over the phone. At the time, I thought nothing of it. I thought of it as a joke. I mean who in their right mind would leave me in charge of a fifteen-year-old girl?"

"Are you saying Mona wasn't..." Mike's tone slips into that of a lawyer.

I shake my head. "She remained lucid until the very end. Even on the pain medications she was aware of who we were and where she was."

I cannot allow him to believe Mona lacked the mental capacity to create a will and guardianship for her daughter. She loved Emma; Emma was her everything.

"Should we go see Emma?" Justin suggests.

My eyes dart to Mike for guidance.

"When do you head back to Iowa City?" he asks.

"A week from today," I answer, hoping he has a plan.

"Does Bonnie still live on the premises?" he inquires, and I nod.

Mike rises, pacing to the window. "Emma buried her mother today. I suggest Bonnie and you set her up in the guest room, show her where everything is, and let her be. Like you, she is mourning. She may choose to stay in her room. Let it be her choice to socialize or be alone. More than likely, she is not ready to talk about living arrangements. Since it is Friday, take a day or two before you discuss it. With Bonnie here, you won't be the only adult. If she wants to talk, there are two of you to choose from."

I nod. When I took a week off from training to return home for the funeral, I did not expect the heavy weight on my shoulders now. I did not plan to hit up a club this weekend, but I did plan to hang with Justin.

"I am heading home," Mike states.

"Want me to stay?" Justin asks.

I shake my head.

"I think she will be more comfortable with only Bonnie and me," I reply.

"Text me if you want me to come over," he offers. "We could order pizza, play pool, and watch a movie. She might like that."

"Maybe tomorrow night," I counter, and he nods before exiting the office with his father.

Now what do I do? Do I walk into the kitchen like any other day? Do I strike up a conversation? Should I ask how she is doing? What did I do when I was fifteen? I camped out in the theater room with video games and movies while I drank the alcohol I snuck from the liquor cabinet.

My stomach flip flops at the thought of Emma drinking away her pain tonight and my new guardian status requiring me to parent the situation. *I am in way over my head.*

Bonnie. I need to talk to Bonnie. She will know exactly what to do. I hesitate at the kitchen doorway, attempting to compose myself. Although I have no clue what to do, I plan to appear like I do. One step through the door Bonnie and Emma turn their heads in my direction.

Before her mother's funeral today, the last time I saw Emma she was thirteen. It was two years ago, at her grandfather and my mother's funerals. I did not see much of her; it was at the beginning of the Covid-19 pandemic, we all wore masks and kept our distance. She barely resembles the girl she did prior to 2020.

Sitting on the stool at the kitchen island, Emma's long legs nearly reach the floor now. Her red-rimmed eyes reveal her sadness from her mother's funeral. She lost her chubby cheeks and gained at least ten inches of hair. Once her brown hair was darkened to almost black. Now it is light brown hair that no longer announces her love of all things goth. She still wears the black slacks and short-sleeve, dark-gray top she wore to the funeral, but it looks like she changed from dress shoes into black high-top Converse. Then again, maybe she wore them to the funeral. *She is not the girl I remember.*

"Would you like to join us for a snack?" Bonnie asks.

I shake my head, pulling a bottle of water from the refrigerator instead. I lean my back against the counter near the fridge, and Bonnie stands between us.

"Should we show Emma to her room?" I inquire, keeping my eyes only on Bonnie.

"I know where the guest rooms are," Emma mumbles.

I nod, realizing this was her grandfather's house her entire life, and she is familiar with its layout. *So much for seeming like I had my shit together.*

"I'm going to go watch a movie," she informs, slipping off her stool.

She leaves the room, pop can in hand, without a backward glance. As soon as she moves out of earshot, I move in front of Bonnie.

Keeping my voice low, I ask, "What do I need to do?"

Bonnie places her hands on my shoulders with a slight smile.

"She'll be fine; it will all be fine," she promises. "She needs…"

"That's just it, I have no idea what she needs. The only thing I know about teenage girls is how to tempt them to have a one-night stand with me," I confess.

"Phish," she swats my chest. "You are her family, and she is not a baby. She needs to stay here, she needs people to talk to about her mother's death when she is ready, and she needs to feel like this is her home. You can give that to her."

"I…"

She interrupts me, "You are mourning, too. Take a day or two. Arrangements for her don't need to be made right now. She has a familiar place to stay, all will be fine."

PROLOGUE
EMMA

It seems the only thing that has not changed in my grandfather's house is Bonnie. Gone are the family photos, upholstered drapes, and large floral arrangements. Many surfaces are bare. *I wonder if Tag simply ordered Bonnie to box everything up and never took the time to redecorate.* The decor was never kid-friendly, but now it is simply depressing.

I search the cabinets below the movie screen in search of the throw pillows and blankets that used to sleep on the reclining theater seats. I desperately need something to wrap around me. Stepping back into the downstairs hallway, I find Bonnie walking towards me with a tray of food and beverages in hand.

"I thought you might enjoy a snack," she says in a low, sweet tone.

Great. More adults treating me like I am made of glass. They expect me to fall apart any second. Mom's second bout with breast cancer lasted over two years. As the months passed, the once vibrant, fun-loving woman dwindled into a frail, over-medicated waif. I began mourning her death a year ago, on the day Mom was diagnosed with a broken arm not caused by a fall or injury. The adults would not tell me, but I knew that meant the cancer would win its war. I witnessed her in so much pain that I think it is a blessing that her body finally gave up. She feels no more pain; her suffering has ended. Inside, I celebrate that.

"Were you looking for something?" Bonnie asks, placing the tray on the counter along the sidewall of the theater room.

"Where do you store the pillows and blankets now?" I ask in return.

Bonnie nods slightly, toddling into the hall. I follow behind her jolly figure, watching as she opens the two large doors built into the wall, swiftly pulling the missing items from a shelf.

"With Tag away at college I tucked them in here to keep them dust free," she explains, extending them to me. "Please use the intercom system if ever you need to find anything. This big old house sits empty most of the year, so things might not be exactly where you remember them."

Her warm brown eyes are a welcome sight on this day of upheaval. I have fond memories of Bonnie from my visits here prior to the pandemic. *This might not be all bad with her still working here.*

"I placed fresh linens in the red guest room at the end of the upstairs hallway. There are toiletries in the attached bath, fresh batteries in the remotes, and I took the liberty of stocking its mini fridge with bottles of water and your pop."

Her hands move from her hips to cross in front of her buxom chest, and then back to her sides. *She is uncomfortable; I make her uncomfortable. I am now a fifteen-year-old freak to be treated with kid gloves.* I fight the urge to roll my eyes. I remind myself she is a sweet woman and is only trying to help me.

"Thank you," I respond. "I think I will crash in here, watching a couple of movies."

"Alright, sweetheart. You know how to reach me should you need me," she smiles wide, waves, and returns upstairs to her household tasks.

I settle into the black leather seat in the center of the front row, take the remote in hand, and press play on a romcom I have watched a handful of times. The title sequence barely rolls when my cell phone pings a text alert. I press pause on the remote.

RACHEL

so how is it?

ME

fine

RACHEL

nope. not gonna cut it. how is it?

ME

weird

Bonnie is (thumb up emoji)

Tag is (thumb down emoji)

RACHEL

is he hot? I bet he's hot

he looks fine in football uniform

ME

gag, he's my step uncle

RACHEL

I'm not related to him

ME

you r never allowed 2 visit me

RACHEL

I'll be good

ME

since when

RACHEL

gotta go bell rang.

I'll call after school

ME

(okay emoji)

I toss my phone in the cup holder and press play on my movie. *Will this be my new life, Bonnie fixing meals and keeping house, Tag ignoring me, and me watching movies or hiding alone in my room?*

Three months. If I endure this for three months then I will turn sixteen. I can look into details of emancipation of a minor, get a car, and live in my mom's house by myself. I will talk to Tag tomorrow, lay the groundwork. He doesn't want me here. Surely he will approve to get me out of his hair.

I miss my books, I miss my kitchen, I miss my house, and... I miss Mom.

PROLOGUE

TAG

I shut my laptop, releasing a deep breath. My summer course load looms less than a week away. *I do not want to be here right now. I need to be on campus; I need my routine, to return to my football workouts, and get back to class. There is no way I can stay here all week. And no way I am taking her to live in my house in Iowa City. Nothing cramps a single guy's style like taking care of a 15-year-old girl. Nope. She is not returning to campus with me. Think. Think. Three years. What am I going to do with Emma until she turns eighteen?*

With football season, off-season workouts, and my extra coursework towards my double major, I cannot drive back and forth to Des Moines. No one lives here; Bonnie keeps the house in my absence.

Bonnie. Bonnie's a mother; Kate is eighteen and headed to college in the fall. Maybe... I need to talk to Bonnie and Barry. If I offer to let the entire family live in the apartment over the garage, maybe they will agree to care for Emma while I attend college for the next two years. She will be seventeen when I move back in; she will not need me to take care of her by then.

1

EMMA

I roll my eyes when Tag enters the kitchen.

"No need to make me dinner tonight," he informs Bonnie as she unloads the dishes from the dishwasher. He pulls a water bottle from the refrigerator. "I'm working in my home office today. Please send Phoebe in when she arrives at nine," he calls over his shoulder on his way out.

"I saw that," Bonnie states, pointing a fork at me from her stance opposite me at the kitchen island.

"Saw what?" I play dumb.

"Don't play coy," she chides. "I saw you roll your eyes when he walked in. What is that all about?"

"He's dressed in his designer suit, complete with French cuffs, alligator shoes, and flashy cufflinks," I state what she already knows. "He is dressed over the top for working in the home office today." I point the top of my to go travel mug in her direction as I speak.

Bonnie shakes her head at me. "Tag worked hard to get to where he is. He has many prestigious clients and must dress accordingly."

I want to argue about Tag working hard to get where he is, but I can't. Although he inherited this mansion and half of my grandfather's estate when his mother and my grandfather passed away during the pandemic, he did attend college and puts in long hours here and at the firm. He continues to work when he has the option to travel the world, partying it up as a playboy with his inheritance the rest of his life.

Tag's attire screams "look at me" and "I'm uber successful". For him, a solid black or navy suit will not do; he opts for pinstripes and bright-colored shirts. *I swear he polishes his cufflinks and the buckles on his shoes daily. Take that back. He probably instructs his household staff to buff them. Sometimes I wonder if anything hides underneath his pretentious exterior.*

Tag

Walking to my office, I cringe at the sight of her in the kitchen. I swear Emma goes out of her way to ensure my misery; it feels like she hammers bamboo sticks under my fingernails. Her ragged black skinny jeans—a splinter under my thumb nail. Her over-sized, faded black Lost Boys tee—a splinter under the nail of my index finger. Her torn and frayed, black Converse high-top shoes—a splinter under another nail. The multitude of dark bracelets on her right wrist and the black nail polish on her left hand—yet another splinter under my nail.

She strives to look as if she could care less about her appearance; when I believe she plans every detail based on eliciting a negative reaction from me. I can't fathom why she seeks to unnerve me so.

I instructed my personal assistant to fill half her closet with appropriate attire, yet she purposely avoids them all. I asked Bonnie to speak with her on many occasions; even she cannot persuade Emma. *The girl will be the death of me.*

2

EMMA

As is always my reaction, I stiffen when Tag walks into the kitchen. Beside me, Rachel squeezes my thigh under the counter in silent support. Mentally, I scroll through my recent actions and upcoming events, searching for any reason he might scorn me. I seem to be a constant embarrassment to him; my mere presence irritates him.

My eyes watch his back at the refrigerator as he pulls out a bottle of water, taking a sip, then turns to face Bonnie.

"What is planned for dinner?" He asks, smiling sweetly in her direction at the stove.

His open fondness for Bonnie confounds me. Towards her, he is the opposite of how he is towards me. From the moment I moved in, he has attempted to avoid me at all costs. On the rare occasion he must interact with me, his cold, distant, and frustrated demeanor conveys his distaste for everything about me.

Closing my eyes, I draw in a long, quiet breath. Memories of our past interactions flood my brain. He vocalized his disdain for my mother's car; not letting me park it in the drive where the neighbors might see it. He insisted that I leave my public school with all my friends to attend the prestigious Catholic high school, and he attempted to force me to wear expensive, trendy clothes, instead of my wardrobe heavy-ladened with black. My presence and appearance enraged him, on the rare occasions he came home from college for my first two years here, and more often now that he lives here full time.

When I open my eyes, Tag no longer stands in the kitchen, Bonnie places a pan in the oven, and Rachel taps on her cell phone. I release the breath I didn't know I held. *Shew. I dodged that bullet.* I mark this up as a rare occasion that he did not express his frustration with everything about me.

3

EMMA

Bonnie knocks on my open bedroom door. In my over-stuffed chair, I lay my Kindle in my lap, turning toward her.

"It's time," she announces, a thin smile upon her face.

I cringe. It's no surprise; Tag's assistant informed me earlier this week about his insistence of my being home today for these appointments. I do not want to go to this work dinner with Tag tonight, I do not want to get my hair styled, and I do not want a manicure. I am only doing this because Bonnie talked me into it. She says this dinner is important. *If it is so important, why is Tag taking me as his plus one? I am sure Pheobe would gladly cling to his arm all evening. Argh!*

"They are set up in the guest room downstairs," Bonnie informs before returning to the kitchen.

I reluctantly trudge my way downstairs, not looking forward to the upcoming hours of primping forced upon me. I realize my day-to-day style is not appropriate for this evening's dinner, but I am perfectly capable of finding my own clothes, styling my own hair, and painting my own nails. I find it asinine to spend hundreds of dollars for in-home salon treatment that I can do myself or ask for Rachel's assistance.

Two women in medical field scrubs greet me with wide smiles. I paste a fake smile upon my face as I enter the makeshift salon.

Tag has a standing appointment every two weeks for his manicurist and hairstylist to come to the house. On more than one occasion as our paths crossed in the kitchen, he made it very clear that the chipped polish on my fingernails drives him nuts, and he detests my choice of dark nail polish to match my black wardrobe.

Sitting in the grooming chair and closing my eyes, the memory of Tag claiming he cannot allow me to meet the guys from the firm looking like he does not take care of me plays in my mind. He acts as if my choice of clothing, nail polish, and hair style reflect poorly upon him. *Just because I do not require thousands of dollars per month to achieve my looks, doesn't mean… I look homeless.*

4

EMMA

Pompous ass.

I shut my bedroom door with a bit more force than I intended and jump at the loud sound.

Arrgghh! Why is he all up in my business? Why can't he live his life and let me live mine? He doesn't need to tell me how to dress, what to do, or how to act.

I don't want to go to a stuffy dinner with the old men from Tag's financial firm. I release a growl. *He never asked me to be his plus one to anything, why now?*

I imagine the entire evening will be the partners who worked with my grandfather, blowing smoke up Tag's entitled ass. I'm tired of everyone revering him as a celebrity, talking about his illustrious high school and D-I college quarterback career. Now he owns my grandfather's firm, with that comes status in Des Moines and most of the state. I wait for the day I witness him using his celebrity status to pass out his autographs. *I don't want to go to a dinner with him.*

"You have to go to college," he has told me more than once. "Everyone of a certain means goes to college whether they use the degree or not. You should take pride in yourself and better yourself by going to college."

I cringe at the memory of him trying to force his prideful ways upon me. Between going to college and driving an acceptable car, he constantly tries to force me to bend to his way. So far, I've been successful in digging in my heels and holding strong to my wishes.

I don't want to go to a dinner with him, let alone dress up to his standards for the dinner. God's gift to women, worships his body. He keeps a nutritionist and personal trainer on staff. He is the poster boy for gorgeous men, but his dick-head personality voids his good looks. In addition to his fake tan, he constantly works out, immaculately styles his hair, requires routine manicures and haircuts, and allows his stylist and personal shopper to buy his designer attire. Believing they are an extension of him, he constantly upgrades his vehicles, except his prized Ducati and Maserati. *I will never live up to his standards. I bet this dinner will last over two hours. What did I do to deserve this punishment?*

5

EMMA

Stupid! Stupid and asinine! The next day, I stand in front of my full-length mirror, detesting my reflection. *This is not me; it couldn't be farther from the real me if it tried.* The silky red dress and matching red heels scream "look at me." I scowl at my reflection. I prefer to blend in rather than stand out.

It's a perfectly fine dress for others, with its sleeveless A-line fit and flared skirt falling just above the knee. I'd much rather wear pants. My preferences in the dress department fall more along the lines of Audrey Hepburn and Jackie Kennedy's style of fashion, paired with a Mary Jane style heel.

Tag cannot make me wear this tonight. I'm eighteen-years-old, and I'll damn well wear what I please. I stomp back into my closet, walking past the first rack containing the clothes I feel most comfortable in and Catholic school uniforms. I slip off the red heels, leaving them on the carpet where they fall. I flip through the hangers along the back wall; these dresses were purchased under Tag's order, by his personal assistant.

No. No. No. Maybe. No. No. Hell no. Maybe. Maybe. Ugh! I let out an exasperated sigh. *I must find… hmm. This might just work.* I pull the hanger from the rod, holding the black capris at arm's length. *What top? Top. Top. Top. Ah-ha!*

I stand in front of my tri-fold mirror, black pedal pushers held from my waist and the three-quarter-length-sleeved, white cardigan set at my shoulders. *Perfect!*

Fearing Tag's reaction if I am not in the library at precisely five o'clock, I scurry to slip off the red dress. Finishing off my new ensemble, I step into a pair of white ballet flats, and my mother's pearl choker. I snag a buffalo plaid hairband, quickly slide it in my hair, and hurry toward the library.

Tag

I glance at my wrist one more time; she's four minutes late. *Of course she's late. Why must she defy me every step of the way?* I step to the library door, prepared to climb the stairs, but she is there. She stands on the first step, beginning her descent. *What happened to the dress my PA procured for this evening? This is yet another way she refuses to follow directions.*

"You look lovely, dear," Bonnie greets, peeking her head from the kitchen.

Emma's cheeks pink, and she grins shyly.

"Ready?" She asks, not waiting for my response as she strides past me toward the garage.

"I was ready four minutes ago," I growl under my breath, following her as I straighten the cuffs of my sleeves beneath my suit jacket.

Fuming at her defiance, I choose to make a call rather than make awkward conversation in the car. Emma fidgets quietly in her seat while I conduct business during our fifteen-minute drive to Hannigan's house.

"Who will be here tonight?" She asks nervously when I park the car.

I huff, having shared this information with her last week when we added the dinner to our calendars. "The three partners from the firm," I speak slowly, hoping she'll retain the information this time. "Peterman, Hannigan, and Lippman. It's Hannigan's house."

With Emma's nod, we exit my Lexus. I motion for her to walk beside me and send up a silent prayer that she will not embarrass me this evening in front of my colleagues.

Emma

I survive the delicious three-course dinner Mr. Hannigan's private chef prepares, while speaking when asked a question, and remaining silent as the four men discussed the firm.

"Shall we retire to the study?" Hannigan suggests.

We rise simultaneously, and I'm surprised as Tag pulls my chair out and ushers me like a gentleman. He puts on quite a show this evening, acting as if the two of us do not avoid each other at all costs.

I sit in the chair Tag pulls out for me at the small oval conference table. Once seated, the four men join me. A server hovers nearby, the men place drink orders, but I decline.

"The lady will have a water," Tag instructs.

If I take another sip, I will explode; the urge to pee hit me over thirty minutes ago. My hope is to end this night and return safely home before I need to use the restroom. Judging from the large binders on the table in front of each of us, it may be hours before I escape.

Once the beverages are delivered, Mr. Hannigan nods at the waiter who exits, closing the double doors behind him.

"Let's begin," he states.

"Emma, what lies before you is the current report of your financial holdings, trusts, and accounts," Mr. Peterman shares.

I open the binder's heavy cover, flipping through several pages. A heavy weight falls hard to the bottom of my stomach, my hands shake, and head to toe I am on fire.

"Excuse me," I croak, rising from my seat.

The four men rise, Tag quickly pulls my chair backwards, and I exit the room as fast as I can without coming off as rude. Through the door, I look one way then the other. Sensing my distress a nearby server points to the left. I scurry in that direction, finding the restroom.

The door closed behind me, I lean my back against it, struggling to breathe. *Water. I need water.* At the sink, I wet a nearby towel, pressing it to my forehead, cheeks, and the back of my neck. I cup a handful of cold water, sipping it in an attempt to calm my queasy stomach. I am unable to stop my tears.

I startle, a squeak escaping, as three raps sound against the wooden door. I turn off the running water.

"Just a minute, please."

"Ma'am, may I fetch you anything?" A female voice asks.

"No thank you, I'm fine," I lie.

Fine. I'm not fine. I was blindsided—shocked to my core. I am anything but fine.

Tag

I fight rolling my eyes at Peterman for the third time since Emma left the room. These three men are not concerned at all by Emma's long exit from our presence.

"I'm going to check on Emma," I state, rising from the table, interrupting their conversation.

Not finding her in the hallway, I make my way down the corridor. A female server rounds the corner, a tray of fresh drinks in her hand.

"Pardon me," I ask for her attention. "Have you seen Emma?"

The server doesn't speak, simply pointing to white French doors.

"Thank you."

Why is she outside? I squeeze through the slightly opened door into the warm night breeze.

"Emma," I call, not wanting to scare her as I approach from behind.

She doesn't turn around, she remains at the stone railing, looking out over the garden. I place my forearms on the stone beside her. Several quiet moments pass, admiring the lush garden in the pale moonlight. I am unsure why she fled and how to proceed.

"Are you okay?" I murmur.

Emma nods, wiping tears off her cheeks with both hands. I welcome the fresh air. Hannigan's study smells of cigars.

"Emma, I need you to tell me what happened," I prompt, knowing I am ill-equipped to handle this situation.

"I had no idea," her shaky voice squeaks. "Seeing Grandfather and Mom's names on the sheets with those numbers…" Emma sobs.

On its own my body moves behind her, wrapping my arms around her. In my hold, her shoulders shake as she trembles.

"Shh," I soothe, my mouth against her hair. "Shh…we can stay out here as long as you need."

Emma spins in my arms, resting her head against my chest. *She is crying. I have never dealt with a crying female. I do not do relationships for this reason.* On its own, one hand begins stroking up and down her back while the other continues holding her to me. Her head under my chin, the fruity scent of her shampoo tickles my nostrils.

"I… I… wanna go home," she sobs.

I tighten my hold on her. "Let's go."

Let's go? Did I really agree to help her escape? Where did that come from? I usher her inside, toward the front door.

"Let me…" I point toward the closed doors to the study. "I will make an excuse and be right back."

Who am I? When did I learn to console a woman and act chivalrous? I only had one glass of scotch, so I can't blame it on the alcohol.

"Are you cold?" I reach for the air conditioner fan control until Emma shakes her head.

We ride the rest of the drive home in silence. Emma seems lost in her thoughts, and I am at a loss—not sure what to say or do. I follow her lead, remaining quiet for the ride, and quietly enter the house.

In the kitchen, I open the refrigerator door. "Would you like a water?" I extend my hand holding a bottle.

Emma shakes her head, plopping onto a stool at the kitchen island.

"I thought you were kicking me out of the house..."

Emma's words freeze me in place, refrigerator door still open.

"What?" *I had to hear her wrong.*

"I thought the point of tonight's dinner was for Hannigan to force me out of your house," she explains.

My mouth opens and closes like a guppy, no words escaping.

"As my eighteenth birthday approaches, I began avoiding you so you couldn't get rid of me," she confesses. "Tonight, I thought my stay of execution was over."

Shaking off my stunned reaction, I close the refrigerator door. I place my palms on the marble between us, leaning towards Emma.

"This is not my house," I state. "It is *our* house. It has always been our house."

She tilts her head, confused.

"When your grandfather passed away, he left it to your mother and me," I say. When she looks more confused, I continue. "Didn't your mother tell you?"

Emma shakes her head, tears welling again. *Please don't cry. Please don't cry.*

"I... I didn't know about..." she blows out a loud puff of air. "I only flipped through a few pages, but what I saw... I did not know about... any of that." She waves her hand through the air.

I shake my head in disbelief. *I'm not buying it; I'm not sure what game she's playing.*

"When you moved in, your lawyer and I shared your mother's will with you," I remind her. "The three of us were in my office."

Emma shakes her head again, tears now flowing down her cheeks, and her lip trembling.

Her trembling lip. It is the same trembling lip the 15-year-old version of her displayed on that day. In my mind I see the bloodshot, red-rimmed eyes of the crying teen I gained custody of years ago. Her entire body shook, and she looked so small, her arms wrapped around her knees, pulling them tight to her chest in my office chair as the lawyers spoke. Only now I realize, she was too upset to listen to everything we threw at her that day.

I shake my head; *I'm an idiot—a thoughtless, selfish, prick.* I was too caught up in college life to pay attention to her needs. By the time I graduated, we were comfortable in our relationship of avoidance. I'd always been on my own; she'd never been alone, and I was not there for her. I left it up to Bonnie to care for her and went about my own life. I did not alert Bonnie to the state of Emma's affairs.

"I can share the Cliff's Notes version now and go through the binder with you when you are ready," I offer, my torso leaning closer to her over the counter.

Emma nods, wiping her tears on a paper towel.

"Your grandfather left control of the firm to me and split his other assets fifty-fifty between your mother and me, including this house." My eyes search hers for signs I should stop or continue.

"When your mother passed, she left everything to you, naming me as trustee until your eighteenth birthday. The title to the house bears both our names; we each own 26% of the shares in the business your grandfather started. Together we own more shares than the other three partners combined. The money your mother inherited along with the money she left you is in your name, and you now have access to all of it," I share.

I gently pinch her chin between my fingers, lifting her gaze from her hands to my eyes.

"I am sorry. I should have prepared you for tonight." I cup her cheek in my hand, and she leans slightly into my palm.

"Even though I thought you knew about your inheritance, I should have talked to you before dinner with the partners." I shake my head.

I handled this wrong for three long years, interpreted her behaviors incorrectly, and was an all-around ass to her. My apology is nowhere near enough. I need to find a way to be better. I am better than this.

"How about I clear some time in my schedule tomorrow for us to go over the binder," I suggest.

Emma nods, causing me to smile slightly at the knowledge I did not screw this up.

6

TAG

This morning, as I sit with my breakfast plate at the kitchen island, I eat slower than normal, delaying my hurry towards my office. My hope is to see Emma before I start my work for the day.

"Bonnie," I call across the room. "When did Emma start drinking coffee for breakfast?"

It is a question I should know the answer to. I knew it was her habit when I returned from college this year. I doubt she drank coffee at age fifteen when she moved in, but I can't be certain.

"The day after her sixteenth birthday she requested I allow her to sip from my morning coffee," Bonnie chuckles, shaking her head. "She hated it, of course, but steadfast in pursuit, she asked me to help her try different varieties of coffee. I made her a cappuccino the next morning."

I bite the inside of my cheek in an attempt not to smile wildly at Emma's tenacity.

"She was never one to eat much at breakfast," Bonnie adds.

Emma enters the kitchen, eyes slightly puffy and bloodshot. *I need to make talking with her today a priority. I should have made it a priority long before now. Oh crap! I hope she did not overhear Bonnie and I talking about her a moment ago.*

"Want some pancakes?" I ask, already knowing her answer.

Shaking her head, she answers, glancing my way, "No thanks, I will stick to my usual cappuccino."

I want to press more; instead, I take another bite of my omelet. Out of the corner of my eye, I watch Emma take her first long sip from her travel mug.

I place a large chunk of omelet and a couple of breakfast potatoes on my now empty toast saucer. Slowly, dramatically, I slide the saucer toward Emma. Her eyes stare at the food, then up to me. Noticing the silence, Bonnie turns from the stove to face us.

"Try a bite," I suggest, unable to fight the smirk forming on my lips. "You wouldn't want Bonnie to think you could not stand her cooking. I personally wouldn't want to be the one that offends Bonnie."

Emma's eyes narrow. She glares at me for a long moment, hoping I will repeal my challenge. I stand resolute, my tongue darting out to wet my lower lip in anticipation.

Bonnie giggles out loud at my antics. I love the jolly sound. A huff escapes Emma's lips as she rises from her barstool.

I can't believe she decides to flee from the kitchen rather than eat two small bites of Bonnie's omelet. I did not peg her for one to back down from a challenge.

Instead of exiting, she opens a drawer on the opposite side of the island from where I sit. I shake my head slightly when she pulls a fork from the dishwasher. I really should know more about where things are located in my own home. Other than my office and my bedroom, I allow Bonnie to do everything for me.

Emma returns to her seat, cuts the chunk of omelet in half and proceeds to take her first bite. I note that Bonnie returns her attention to the griddle once again.

"I'm only eating this because you are forcing me to," Emma mumbles. "It probably won't even taste good with all the guilt you sprinkled onto it. See, here is some. Here is some, and here is some more guilt."

I snort loudly, surprise floods Emma's face as she chews, and Bonnie turns hands on hips watching us.

"How was that guilt?" I ask through my laughter. "Could you taste it or should I add more?"

She nods while chewing, so I take that as a sign to lay on more guilt. "Bonnie enjoys fixing breakfast. She puts lots of love in the first meal of the day. She is a morning person, and you offend her by only ordering a cappuccino," I tease.

Emma holds up her hand palm out, halting me, "Geez, enough."

My laughter continues until my phone alarm reminds me I have a call in ten minutes, and I need to prep for it.

"I will finish this in my office," I inform the women. "Delicious as always, Bonnie." I kiss her cheek. "Emma, it's been a pleasure. I hope you will join us again for the most important meal of the day." With a smirk, I leave.

Emma

I slide the saucer with potatoes away from my seat. Bonnie scrutinizes me.

"What?"

She shakes her head, setting out the fixings to top Barry's pancakes.

I clear my throat. "Bonnie?"

She waves her cooking spatula in hand as she talks, "Whatever that was." She points the spatula from me to where Tag sat. "I love seeing him laugh and tease. He rarely lets his guard down to do it. Whatever happened last night... I hope the two of you have worked through your differences, and this new fun friendship remains. You both need it."

I want to mumble that I am sure the prickish side of him will return by noon. This is a momentary bit of insanity on his part, but Bonnie is happy. I can't cause that to fade.

Thoughts of last night return, washing over my features.

"Hey, what did I say? Why are you near tears?" Bonnie asks.

I fight breaking down as Bonnie hugs me. I begin to open up about the shock of last night. Of course, Tag's perfectly polished assistant arrives to end our moment.

"I don't mean to interrupt, but I need Tag's breakfast plate," she says snidely.

She looks down on Bonnie, treating her like the help of the house, and always makes it clear that she despises my presence.

"Tag already ate," I gripe and shew her away with a flick of my hand.

She is a guest in our house. Well, I guess she is an employee. Anyway, she has no right to treat Bonnie the snooty way she does. On more than one occasion she acted as if she was the Future Mrs. Tag Whatley. I pray that never happens. I am sure her first task would be to fire Bonnie. She is jealous of how close she is to Tag. Her second task would be to kick me out of the house.

Mid-morning I get a text. My eyes must be playing tricks on me.

TAG

my schedule frees up @ 2

taking afternoon off

let's go through binder

I didn't even know he had my number. I guess he pays my cell phone bill, so he has to have it. He hasn't texted or called me once in the past three years.

I know he said he would walk me through the heavy binder full of financial info thrust upon me last night, but I never expected a text from him. I assumed he would send his hoity-toity assistant to deliver his message and push it out a day or two.

7

EMMA

"Thank you," I smile.

Tag sits across his large wooden desk from me, a small smile upon his face. I appreciate the time and patience he shared with me. I now know in great detail my finances.

I am numb; no eighteen-one-year-old should possess such wealth. *Money is not important to me. Of course, only those with money say this.*

"Now, what should we do about dinner?" Tag asks, steepling his hands in front of his chin, drawing my attention to his full lips.

A moment passes before I shake away my sudden interest in his perfect mouth, and process his words. *Dinner?* I'm confused.

"I told Bonnie to take the night off," he shares, proudly smiling. "I thought we could go out or order in."

Dinner? He plans to eat dinner with me? I cannot name the last time he joined me for dinner. Mostly, I joined Bonnie's family for meals to avoid dining alone.

"Umm…" I stammer, unsure how to answer him.

I rise, exiting the office.

"Emma?" Tag calls for my attention, following me.

"Why don't we fix dinner ourselves," I challenge. In the kitchen I search for ingredients.

His brow furrows, while he processes my suggestion. I giggle internally; I know he rarely attempts to fix himself a sandwich, let alone an entire meal.

"I am afraid I am… not skilled in the kitchen," he chuckles.

"Then it's settled," I state, eager to challenge him more. "What shall it be, chicken or pasta?"

When he does not answer, I offer, "I will show you what to do."

"As I am the novice, you choose," Tag offers.

He squirms; I rather enjoy his discomfort. His usual cool indifference slips away, replaced by uncertainty, hesitation, and releasing of his perpetual power.

I pull chicken from the refrigerator, along with asparagus and cherry tomatoes. I grab a skillet, the cast iron griddle, knives—everything I will need to prepare a simple, yet delicious meal.

"Can you grab garlic from the refrigerator?" I ask Tag.

As I unwrap the two chicken breasts, I hear him open the door, then feel the cool air from the refrigerator upon my back.

"What exactly am I looking for in here?" he asks, embarrassed.

I want to laugh. He is twenty-three with no clue what garlic looks like. Instantly, I want to take him grocery shopping; I am sure he is truly a fish out of water in the store. I duck under his arm, standing between him and the shelves, pull open the drawer, and grab the garlic clove. Turning, I dangle it between our faces. He chuckles, shaking his head.

My smile plastered to my face, I am suddenly aware of our closeness. Tag's eyes twinkle with… *Is that humor?* I search my mind for a time I've ever witnessed him smile or laugh.

"Found the garlic," he grins. "What is next?"

I duck under his arms, making my escape.

"What are we making anyway?" he questions.

"Skillet pesto chicken and veggies," I answer, mentally running through the ingredients I might need. "Can you cut the chicken breasts into one-to-two-inch strips?" I prompt, sliding the kitchen shears toward him. "I'll strain the oil off the sun-dried tomatoes and cut the asparagus in half," I inform.

As I complete my tasks, I keep a watchful eye on Tag and his task. He is still cutting the chicken when I begin halving the cherry tomatoes. After slicing two, I realize Tag can complete the tomatoes. I warm olive oil in the skillet.

"Done!" he announces proudly.

I take the cutting board of sliced chicken and direct him to halve the cherry tomatoes.

"What's that?" Tag asks.

"I'm adding a pinch of salt and grinding pepper," I explain. "Now, I'm adding the sun-dried tomatoes."

Tag seems interested, so I explain as I continue to cook. "Now, I'm removing the chicken and tomatoes, leaving the oil behind," I share. "You know what this is right?" I tease as I lay the asparagus in the hot skillet. "I'm adding more…"

"Salt," he deadpans.

I smile at him before continuing, "The rest of the sun-dried…"

"Tomatoes," he finishes for me.

I move the green asparagus sticks around the skillet for about five minutes, slide them onto a platter, and return the chicken back to the skillet, adding pesto to coat it as it reheats. Once warm, I urge Tag to add the cherry tomatoes as I remove the skillet from the heat. I stir before sliding these ingredients with the asparagus on the platter.

"This looks delicious," Tag smiles. "I cannot believe you made this without a recipe."

"We made it," I correct, bumping my shoulder to his. "Grab silverware and let's eat."

I set out two plates and napkins. Back at the island, I watch Tag search drawer after drawer.

Tag

. . .

Where does Bonnie keep the utensils? I open the drawer on either side of the stove. *Nope, not in here.* I peek in the two long drawers near the refrigerator—*not in there.* I release a frustrated sigh as I spin towards the center island. It does not escape me that Emma's biting her lips and fighting a smile. I am glad she enjoys my frustration. *I eat breakfast in the kitchen most mornings. I should pay more attention to Bonnie as she works.* I release a breath I did not know I held when the next drawer I open contains silverware. I place two forks and knives on the counter.

Emma smiles proudly as she passes the serving tongs to me. I place two tong-fulls of chicken, tomatoes, and asparagus upon her plate. I look to Emma; she nods, signaling it is enough. Next, I fill my plate and join her on a barstool.

"When was the last time you fixed yourself a meal?" Emma asks, a forkful paused inches from her mouth.

My eyes lock on her pink lips as she speaks. I force myself to concentrate on her question.

"Other than sports shakes?" I shake my head and smirk.

"Come on…" she protests. "Not even a sandwich?"

"I am pathetic," I state. "Boarding school cooks, take out, nutritionists at the college fitness center, and now Bonnie makes sure I do not starve."

Emma swallows her food before speaking. "Well, now you've officially prepared a real meal." She beams with pride.

I fight the urge to argue she cooked, and I cut up a few things.

Emma

"May I be honest?" I implore.

"Please," Tag urges.

"You don't seem happy," I share, and he flinches at my frankness.

"You work a multitude of hours, constantly barking at everyone around you, never smiling or looking as if you enjoy your work."

Tag's eyes peer through mine, searching the truth I hold deep within my soul. I don't hold back; I allow him to see I firmly believe every word I spoke. I challenge him to listen to me—to truly hear my words.

"Why finance?" I inquire.

Tag's head tilts, and he bites his lips tight between his teeth. I am honored that he ponders his answer. *I hope he intends to answer honestly.*

"When my mother married your grandfather, we moved into this massive house. I was in awe of its size, its pool, and all that his job provided. I was only six, I never knew such things existed." He pulls his eyes from mine, looking up towards the ceiling before continuing.

"I lived here for six months before Mother shipped me off to a boarding school. In that time, I became enamored with his influence and demeanor in all things," Tag shares. "Frank had a daughter he adored, a son-in-law he bragged of, and a baby granddaughter he doted on. I wanted it all—the family and the funds."

My heart bleeds for the young Tag, raised with only his mother, then sent off to school alone. I imagine this house from a six-year-old-boy's eyes; I envision his longing for a family.

"At school, I quickly learned the career paths of prestige. I worked harder than my peers to achieve high marks to earn favor in the eyes of my friends and in Frank's eyes. He began bragging of my scholarly achievements. That fueled my desire to continue and follow in his footsteps," Tag shrugs. "His attention became my drug of choice, and I could not get enough."

"But do you love finance?" I further pry.

"I have an affinity for numbers, the knack for analyzing facts and figures…" he explains.

"There are many jobs for your skills," I state what I am sure he already knows. "Is there another branch of finance that you might enjoy more?"

Tag rolls his eyes. "You are worse than a dog with a bone."

It's my turn to shrug. "I'm stating the obvious, what everyone in this house easily sees. You're not happy, and you deserve to be."

"What about you?" He counters. "If you had known about your inheritance, would you have attended college?"

I shake my head.

"I enjoy cooking and have for as long as I remember," I confess. "My dream is to open my own restaurant as a head chef. To run a successful restaurant, I believe I must know how to perform every job. So far, I bussed tables, washed dishes, served as a hostess, and as a waitress."

"Shouldn't a chef attend a culinary institute?" He asks.

"Maybe, if I aspired to be a world-renowned chef. But I believe hands-on learning will benefit me more for my goals," I explain. "I experimented a lot growing up. Mom was often my Guinea pig," I laugh.

"She told me all about many of your concoctions," Tag chuckles.

I feel my face crinkle. *When did Mom tell him these stories?* I brush off the thought, perhaps he is only being kind.

"I enjoy trying new recipes and techniques I see on tv or the internet," I share. "I am constantly learning.

"If you didn't take over Grandfather's firm, what part of finance might you have explored?" We detoured over to discussing my career path, it's time we return to his.

"If money were not an issue, I think venture capitalist investing in startup companies," he shares, his eyes lighting up with a slight smile upon his lips.

Ah-ha!

"Money is not an issue for you," I remind him. "You should give it a try."

I study his face, observing his doubt fade and a flicker of excitement light it up. My belly warms in hopes I might help Tag find happiness.

"My first venture could be your restaurant," he offers.

I shake my head. "I am not ready for my own place," I state.

"Well, you do not need my money; you can fund your own restaurant anytime you want," Tag chuckles.

"I do think you should look into changing careers," I reiterate. "Your face lights up just discussing it."

"Maybe I will."

His smile grows larger. It warms my heart to know I made him smile more tonight than I witnessed in years.

8

EMMA

I cannot wipe away my silly smile as I wash my face, apply my moisturizer, and brush my teeth before bed. *It is silly—stupid really.* I cannot think that one pleasant evening with Tag means things will change. *Leopards can't change their spots. Is it can't, don't, or won't change? Won't change sounds more like it; men won't change.*

It must be enough to experience this one evening of reprieve in his company. I am sure tomorrow things will return to the status quo. He will return to his flashy, privileged ways, and I will return to avoiding him at all costs.

After slipping under my sheets, I turn out the lamp on my bedside table. Settling into my pillows, my thoughts return to my suggestion Tag look for a career he enjoys. I smirk at the memory of his pupils dilating at my mention of becoming a venture capitalist. Clearly he is interested. *I hope he takes the bait I placed before him tonight.*

Through my windows, the lights of the swimming pool catch my attention. Glancing at the time on my cell phone, I find it past eleven. Tag's late-night swims are common, but usually occur after midnight. *I wonder if this means he is contemplating our conversation.*

Tag

Tonight, I don't keep track of my laps; instead, I stew over Emma's suggestion that I change my career path. My impression of her shattered into a million pieces in the last twenty-four hours. She is not the rebellious thorn in my side I thought her to be. Although she kept her distance, she kept tabs on me through the lens of her microscope.

Once I got past the shock that she observed me and my work, her challenge to look into becoming a venture capitalist pierced my heart. It's as if she peers straight into my soul; she sees I am unhappy, and she longs to change that. I looked down at her, while she truly paid attention to me over the past three years.

My abhorrent behavior towards her led her to avoid me. Her earnest observation and suggestion fills me with guilt. Legally, I served as her guardian, but only on paper. I passed her off to Bonnie, unwilling to spend time with her, learn about her, and be an active part of her life as a guardian should.

At first, I took offense to her refusal of me funding her first restaurant. However, her reasoning endeared me. She was born into money, where I had to prove worthy of inheriting it. While I strive to acquire more in all that I do, she strives to pay her dues rather than use her influence. *I have much to learn about her.*

On my next lap down and back, I ponder her suggestion to find my happiness. If I cannot invest in her restaurant, perhaps I should find another one in the area. Maybe a club would be a better place to begin, or … I fear no number of laps tonight will allow me to make this decision. I need to conduct research, and put out some feelers. After all, Rome was not built in a day.

I hang on the pool's edge, steadying my breath before drying off. As I toss the towel over my shoulder, my eyes halt on Emma's bedroom windows. Her room is dark, causing me to wonder if she is blessed to fall asleep the moment her head touches her pillow. Surely if she struggles to fall asleep, I would find light, shadows, and movement through her windows. *If she sleeps, I am jealous of her ability to shut off her mind and rest.*

9

TAG

"Come in," I call after three knocks upon my office door.

I continue responding to the email currently on my laptop screen, until I hear a throat clear. Looking up, Kate stands across the desk from me. Her dark brown hair forms a ponytail high on her head, while her light makeup accentuates her deep brown eyes. *She leaves for Spain in two days; I wonder if she needs more money.*

"I need five minutes of your time," she states, striding to my side.

The kind of woman that goes after what she wants. Instead of sitting in the chair across the desk from me, Kate takes the mouse from my right hand, quickly moving it, clicking on webpages on my laptop screen. My eyes dart this way and that, attempting to uncover her intentions.

"Watch," she directs, stepping aside as a YouTube video plays full screen before me.

The channel's name is "Talk Foodie To Me." I go to argue, but Emma's wide smile and blue eyes fill the screen. She expertly moves around the kitchen, measuring, and stirring as she talks into the camera.

"Hey," I complain when Kate pauses the video.

On the home page, I notice a long line of videos posted all star-ring Emma.

"I have an idea for Emma's birthday gift this year, but I need your help," Kate announces, now sitting on my desk.

"I am all ears," I chuckle.

My interest is peaked; it is not our habit to go in on a gift for Emma. In fact, I normally send Bonnie to the store to purchase a gift with instructions to leave my name off it.

"Emma's YouTube Channel is rapidly growing. She shoots these videos with only her cell phone. With over 15,000 followers, she needs proper video and audio equipment," she shares.

I raise a brow.

Kate huffs crossing her arms. "It is more than I can afford. Hell, it is more than my parents can afford. That is why I came to you." She pokes my shoulder. "I don't have to tell you she can make money with her channel. Think of it as an investment in her business."

Smiling, I sit back in my chair, crossing my arms across my chest.

"I'll leave it to you," Kate states, hopping off my desk.

"Hey," I protest.

"You are a big boy. I am sure you know someone or can research the lights, microphones, and cameras needed to up her game," she laughs, walking through my office door, waving over her shoulder.

I press play on the next video, taking my cell phone in hand. As I watch, I text, putting this plan in action.

ME
need your help

JUSTIN
I'm (ear emoji)

ME
YouTube Talk Foodie To Me

JUSTIN
(thumbs up emoji)

ME

after work

JUSTIN

(thumbs up emoji)

I watch Emma in video after video, creating dishes in our kitchen in front of the camera as she beams. I am jealous of her love for her chosen field. Food is her passion, and cooking is her superpower. I cannot wait to surprise her with an upgrade for her hobby. She does a fabulous job but deserves more. With our gift, she will turn this hobby into income.

In the next twenty-four hours, I view every one of her videos. Her eyes glimmer with excitement, and she constantly smiles. She shares the history of food and fun facts as she creates each dish. I listen to her tell viewers that garnish is unnecessary but adds a bit of artistic flare to the finished product.

Emma films herself shopping for ingredients and even offers advice to other shoppers near her. I learn that in warm months she shops at the farmers' markets on Saturday mornings and Thursday evenings. She knows many of the vendors by name and asks about their families.

This is much more than a fad or hobby; she truly loves to cook and bake. She wastes her gifts as a waitress and dishwasher at someone else's restaurant. I must do what I can to encourage her. She might not want me to invest in her restaurant, but she cannot return a birthday gift from the four of us.

10

TAG

"Dude, she has over 15,000 subscribers," Justin announces. "That's huge!" he extends his cell phone screen towards me. "And over 600,000 TikTok followers. She should already be making money from both of these companies."

I nod. "We are not focusing on making money for her," I remind him. "We are finding her better equipment to produce her videos."

My friend nods. "I am just pointing out she's already earned enough followers to earn income from this."

"Cameras, lights, filters…" I prod.

"Remember Tank?" Justin asks, tucking his phone back in his pocket.

My brow furrows. The nickname sounds familiar.

"Lineman our junior year," he prompts. "Tank was a tank on and off the field."

I smile at the memories.

"His family owns an AV business in the Quad Cities," Justin divulges.

"Do you think he can…"

"Want me to contact him?" Justin tugs his phone back out.

"Emma's birthday is Saturday. When is she opening presents?" he inquires.

Two things hit me at once. First, Justin knows Emma's birthday. If it were not for the firm needing to divulge the status of her investments, I would not. Second, I should probably invite him to join us for the party. It is only a dinner and gifts, but I intend to enlist Kate's help to make it a celebration.

"Birthday dinner is Saturday evening," I answer. "You will join us, won't you?"

My friend's eyes light up as a slow smile slips upon his face. "Of course," he cheers. "We better hurry if we plan to have her gift set up." He dials his phone, placing the call on speaker.

It surprises me that he saved Tank's phone number. I do not recall ever adding any of my teammate's numbers to my contacts.

Tank is excited to hear from us and states he set up similar equipment for other social media bloggers. He assures us his team can install everything Friday within an eight-hour window, and he plans to bring everything he might need and more. After the call, Tank emails us photos of previous installations and equipment details for us to make selections that best fit our space. As we look at the photos, Justin poses an important question.

"How do you plan to keep it a secret as they install all of this in Bonnie's kitchen?"

Hmm. I want to surprise Emma, but now it does not seem possible. Even if I ask Kate to keep her busy on Friday, she will be in the kitchen multiple times on Saturday.

"You could add an overnight trip and spa day as part of the gift," Justin suggests.

There will be no way to hide all the new cameras in our kitchen.

"If only she had her own kitchen space," I think out loud.

"You have the pool house kitchen," he offers.

Whoa! I should have thought of that.

"Perfect!" I proclaim.

We never have extended house guests that stay in the pool house.

"She will love it! Her own space and the ability to leave her equipment set up to use anytime." Justin stands. "We should send pics of the space to Tank."

I follow him from my office. My excitement grows with every step. I shoot a text as we pass the pool.

ME

meet me in pool house

KATE

on my way

(smiling emoji)

While Justin takes both video and photos, I explain our plan to Kate.

"I sent the stuff to Tank," Justin says, approaching the two of us.

"Thank you," I pat him on the back.

Kate smiles brightly. "I knew you'd help us pull this off," she brags. "Emma's gonna lose her shit."

Eyes closed; I shake my head at her.

"She'll hate it and love it at the same time."

She is right. Emma will detest the amount of money and planning we put into this, but she will be excited to utilize it all.

"Now, how will we keep Emma from seeing the transformation on Friday?" I ask the group.

"Lie," Kate shrugs, as if it is that easy.

"Tell her there was an electrical issue that Barry requested you fix," Justin offers.

"Or... tell her Justin plans to move in, and you're adding surround sound for him," Kate plots.

"That would explain the AV vans in the driveway," Justin agrees.

"You should still arrange for her to leave with her friend for the day," Kate suggests.

"I will leave that part to you," I defer.

Kate winks at me. "This is so cool."

11

TAG

"Where's the birthday girl?" Barry inquires, drinking his coffee at the table.

"I'm here," Emma proclaims, entering the room.

Her wet hair pulled high on her head after her shower, her skin glows from her afternoon spent poolside. The moisturizer on her sun-kissed skin glistens in the kitchen lights. Her red V-neck, cap sleeve t-shirt clings to her chest and waist. Her ripped denim shorts are cuffed at the thighs with strategically placed rips. Her feet are bare, exposing her ruby red nail polish. *This casual look suits her.*

"Where are we going for dinner?" Barry asks, looking up at Bonnie as she stands behind him.

"We're making homemade pizzas," Bonnie answers, smiling down at her husband.

I glance toward Emma to see what she thinks of this menu. Her eyes fly around the kitchen, and she smiles. Bonnie told me Emma enjoys simple family activities. I knew she would like to cook our own meal, but I worried pizza might be too pedestrian for someone with her skill set. *Of course, Bonnie was right.*

"Let's get busy," Rachel encourages, moving to Emma's side.

"Barry and I will work on the barbecue chicken," Bonnie suggests.

"Woman, you know I'm not cooking unless it's on a grill," Barry argues.

Bonnie's hands fly to her rotund hips. "Then… Kate and I will make the barbecue chicken, Tag and Justin will make the Hawaiian, and Emma and Rachel can make the Margherita."

Emma, Kate, Bonnie, and Rachel begin setting up their area and pulling ingredients. Justin and I exchange a knowing look. We have not the foggiest idea where to begin. Justin places his hands on Rachel's shoulders and urges her between us. This forces me to take a step in Emma's direction.

"If we want to eat this pizza, Tag and I cannot be partners," Justin chuckles.

Emma places the back of her hand over her mouth in an attempt to hide her giggles.

"Tell me what to do," I urge, not wanting to fall behind the other groups.

"Hold out your hand," she orders and pours a quarter-sized dollop into the palm of my hand.

"Coat your fingertips and spread the crust lightly over the entire baking stone," she directs.

I nod, beginning my assigned task. Beside me, Emma ladles a scoop of tomato sauce in the center of the dough.

"Please use the back side of the spoon to spread the sauce within half an inch of the edge."

Next, she drizzles more olive oil over the sauce.

"Now scatter some basil on the sauce," she instructs.

I nervously do as told, hoping I have the correct ratio.

"Umm…" Kate points at our pizza. "Doesn't the basil go on top?" She raises her eyebrows.

"Emma told me to put the basil on now…" *Right?* I am sure she did. I do not want to mess this up.

Emma places her hand upon my shoulder as she speaks. "I find if you place basil under the cheese, the heat of the wood-fire oven doesn't incinerate it."

I replay Emma's words, hoping her assuring hand on my shoulder means I did not screw up.

"Never, and I mean never, doubt Emma," Barry tells his daughter from his seat across the room. "She's a better cook than your mom." Not wanting to offend his wife, he approaches Bonnie, placing a kiss on her plump cheek. "You know I love your cookin'," he murmurs low. "But that girl could make a cowpie taste good."

The room bursts into laughter. I watch Emma, unsure if his comment about cow feces is a compliment. When she blows him a kiss with a wink, I realize he loves her cooking.

"Why do they get the pizza oven?" Kate whines to her mom.

"Ours will be on a stone in this oven." She points to Justin and Rachel. "Theirs will go on the grill, and all will be delicious." Bonnie informs her daughter and beams at each of us.

"Whatever." Kate rolls her eyes. "Text me when dinner is ready," she assumes her seat by her father at the table with her attention one hundred percent on her cell phone screen. Bonnie brushes it off as no big deal, returning to her pizza.

"Now what?" I whisper for only Emma to hear.

Emma passes me white clumps of cheese. "We need to break this mozzarella into large chunks over the top of our pizza," she demonstrates as she speaks.

I follow her lead. To my right, Justin and Rachel whisper and laugh as they assemble their assigned pizza. Rachel constantly touches him as she talks. My best friend certainly seems to enjoy her attention.

"Tag," Emma's voice interrupts my observation.

"Hmm?" I ask.

Emma's dazzling smile warms me. "Please carry the pizza out to the wood oven," she directs, before leading the way toward the patio.

I quickly scoop up the pizza and follow. Barry sits with a mixed drink at a nearby patio table after starting the oven and grill for us. Emma places our pizza in the wood-fire oven. I watch Rachel and Justin struggle to maneuver their pizza and stone onto the grill.

Emma's shoulder bumps mine. "We did good," she smiles. "We make a good team."

Her words level me. I avoided Emma at all costs for three years for no good reason. She is not the brat I believed her to be. She likes working with me and has the patience of a saint to do so. Lost in my thoughts, before I know it, Emma's pulling the pizza from the oven.

"Here, let me," I offer, placing my hands by hers on the long wooden handle of the pizza paddle. I barely breathe as I follow her to the kitchen. Our pizza resembles one from the cover of a food magazine or ad. It definitely does not look homemade. *This is all Emma. I may have helped, but it was her constant supervision that enabled this outcome.* I am proud to present her finished product to our group. I place the pizza on the island near the two other pies. Bonnie forces plates into our hands, prompting us to fill them as we admire our work.

Full plate in hand, I take a seat between Justin and Emma. Bonnie and Barry sit opposite us with Kate and Rachel at each end of the table. Between bites and praising the flavors, conversation flows. I listen intently as Rachel and Emma talk about their recent golf outing and their volunteer hours each Sunday at the animal shelter. I learn more about Emma with each passing minute.

12

EMMA

No gifts. I see no gifts. *Finally, my family and friends honor my wishes for no presents on my birthday.* Internally, I smile as I swallow my last bite of salad. I detest celebrating myself; tonight, we celebrate our friendships and I absolutely love it. I prefer to focus on our time together instead of the pressure of opening gifts and reacting appropriately to each. I'm more relaxed, and I love it.

I stand gathering plates.

"Uh-huh," Kate argues.

"Birthday girls do *not* do dishes," Justin announces.

"Dessert and dishes later," Kate states, standing with hands on her hips.

I quirk a brow at Justin when he approaches, waving a black cloth at me.

"We have a birthday surprise for you," he informs, a gigantic smile on his tan face.

My eyes dart to Bonnie and Barry; they shrug as they smile wide.

"Put on your blindfold," Kate orders. "We have one big present for you."

My stomach plummets. *"One big present"—that scares me more than four presents. This means it is expensive. Tag better not have purchased the*

43

new car he's tried to force upon me for years. The blindfold adds to my anxiety. It adds more pressure for my reaction to meet the givers' excitement. I fight a shudder as Justin ties the blindfold.

"Let me help you hop on Tag's back," Justin urges, hands at my waist.

With my eyes covered, I cannot see where anyone stands.

"I can walk," I argue.

"We don't want you to trip," Bonnie counters.

"Piggyback or he can carry you," Justin murmurs near my ear, causing goosebumps on the exposed skin of my neck.

Quickly, I decide Tag carrying me seems too intimate.

"I guess piggyback," I say through a sigh. I reprimand myself; they are excited about this.

"Hop on; let's go." Tag's voice encourages, approaching me from the front.

Justin's hands at my hips tighten. "Hop on three," he states. "1,2,3."

My hands on Tag's shoulders, I hop and Justin places me safely against Tag's back. His woodsy scent floods my nostrils as my arms wrap tightly around his neck.

"Can't breathe," he rasps.

I loosen my grip while his laughter vibrates against my chest. I'm not sure what's gotten into him lately. I like this new, playful, often-smiling side of Tag. I don't care if he's been tolerable; if he bought me a car, I'm gonna lose my shit.

The warm, humid evening air signals we've stepped outside. The trickling sound of water alerts me we are in the backyard, not the driveway. I breathe a small sigh of relief as it can't be a vehicle if we are out here.

"If you toss me in the pool, I will get even," I proclaim.

Tag chuckles, "You really don't trust me, do you?" he scoffs.

"I am blind-folded, on your back," I remind him.

"I won't let anything happen to you," Rachel states from behind me.

I hear a door open and sense us stepping into the pool house. *Is Tag moving me from the main house into the pool house? Breathe. I must not over-react in front of Bonnie and Barry.* I'm lost in my own thoughts when I am lowered to the floor. The blindfold slips from my head and bright lights assault my eyes. *It's too bright. It's not normal.* I blink rapidly, attempting to focus through watering eyes. *What the...?* The kitchen area contains new lights in every direction. Craning my neck, I spot black cameras mounted everywhere I look. Kate and Rachel guide my shoulders on a tour deeper into the space. The former stove and fridge have been replaced by commercial-grade steel appliances. On the counter, I find the pots and pans I've coveted over a year now. Suddenly, it hits me. Tears flood my eyes. *The extra lighting... the mounted cameras...* I slowly spin in place. *New appliances... new cookware... new countertop appliances.* I notice the cameras follow my movements from all sides. *It's a studio.* My hands fly to my mouth, a hiccup escapes, and tears trail down my cheeks.

"You guys." I fan my face.

"Let's film us making tonight's dessert," Bonnie suggests.

I realize now a batch of cupcakes sit atop a cooling rack on the counter, and ingredients litter the side counter.

"We thought we could make a batch from scratch and decorate the one's Mom already made," Kate grins.

"We'll film tonight, and you can edit then post it tomorrow," Rachel shares.

"It's amazing." I hug Bonnie.

"This was all Tag," she states.

"Nah," Tag argues. "Kate approached me with this idea, Bonnie knew which appliances and cookware to buy, and Justin knew a guy for all the tech gadgets."

I love that everyone helped, but it doesn't escape me that Tag paid big bucks to make all this happen.

"Thank you, everyone," I say through tears.

Tag

· · ·

My chest swells, witnessing Emma laugh as she bakes a batch of cupcakes. Justin and I hang back with Barry, while the women take turns assisting Emma.

"Tag and Justin," Emma calls a large, sweet smile upon her face, and her eyes twinkle in the lights. "The two of you get to help me decorate cupcakes."

I want to argue; I would much rather watch her than join her on camera.

"Let's go, bro," Justin encourages, slapping me on the back.

"One of you on each side," she prompts.

"Aprons," Rachel reminds us through laughter.

As I lift it over my head and tie the black apron around my waist, I glance frequently towards Emma to make sure I am doing it correctly. Emma trails her fingertips across the embroidered letters decorating my chest.

"Whose idea was it to put my blog name on the aprons?" she inquires.

"That was me," Rachel brags.

"Thank you," Emma beams. "I love it."

"We knew you would," Kate explains.

The sound of the whipped cream spray can draws everyone's attention to Justin on Emma's other side. White fluff paints his lips.

"He's such a man child," Kate laughs.

"You have to keep that in your footage," Rachel giggles.

I shake my head at my friend's antics for attention.

"Okay, guys," Emma begins. "Choose between icing and whipped cream to decorate your tops." She holds a bottle in one hand and a device in her other. "For icing, you may use these icing applicators. They have different tips for designs. Or," she wiggles her right hand. "You can use a rubber spatula to apply icing."

I am so out of my element here. Justin plays around in his kitchen with his mom from time to time, while I don't even know the name of the rubber thing she mentioned.

"I'm skilled with whipped cream," Justin suggestively states. He aims the nozzle and sprays white fluff on top of his two cupcakes.

I feel Emma's eyes on my face.

46

"You think you can teach me how to ice these?" I challenge, hoping she will demonstrate what I need to do.

"Tag's favorite color is blue," Emma says into the camera. "I am adding three drops of sky-blue food coloring and one drop of violet. As I stir it becomes this deep navy-blue color. It's perfect for a masculine design for Tag."

I watch as she scoops the icing into a plastic bag and secures a tip on it.

"Practice on this surface," she directs, tapping her finger on a piece of paper. "Gently squeeze the bag as you move the nozzle." She demonstrates with a bag of cherry red icing on two cupcakes before her. "Make lines like these or make dollops like these."

Both techniques look difficult to me.

"Maybe I should use the rubber," I offer.

Justin chortles with Kate and Rachel joining in.

"It's not a rubber," he laughs. "It's a rubber spatula."

I shrug, and icing leaks from my bag onto one of my cupcakes.

"Ahh," I groan.

"Oopsie," Emma sing-songs. "No worries." Using her finger, she erases my faux pas. "See? It's good as new. Go ahead. If you don't like it, we can wipe it clean and start over."

Emma is a terrific teacher. I see why followers are drawn to her. I take my time, placing dollops upon dollops on my cake top. It looks better than I expected. Slowly, I raise my eyes to find hers smiling back at me.

"That's great!" she champions. "Try a different design on your next one."

When she turns her attention to Justin, I instantly miss it. I enjoy her attention and instruction, probably more than I should

13

EMMA

I was reluctant to leave my new studio space. *Studio space. I have my own kitchen recording space.* I'm gobsmacked. Never in a million years would I have created such a space for myself. I absolutely love that my family and friends joined together to create such a perfect gift. I plan to use it every chance I get. This raises my cooking videos on so many levels.

Rachel fell asleep fast. I assume it's due to the alcohol she consumed with Kate while we watched two movies this evening. Justin and Tag joined us for one movie before leaving us to watch our rom-com. I declined Kate's offer of alcohol. Rachel and I are underage, and while I'm not a prude, I was not in the mood tonight. I'm still flying high from my new kitchen.

Try as I might, I cannot turn off my brain tonight. Rachel's light snoring grates at my nerves. I look to my nightstand for my cell phone. I need to make a list of recipes for my upcoming videos. *It's not here.* I try to recall when I last used it. *The pool house.*

I slip from my bedroom, descending the main staircase. I hear loud noises from the kitchen. I pause at the door. Justin chases a plastic water bottle across the floor on his hands and knees. The open refrigerator doors light the room. *He's drunk.* I close my eyes tight and draw in a long breath for patience.

"Justin," I call as I approach.

"Em," he slurs.

"Can I help you?" I ask.

He halts his attempts of grasping the bottle and rises.

"I'm thirsty."

I pass him a bottle of water from the fridge before shutting the doors. The room darkens, but for the faint lights from the beneath the lower cabinets at floor level.

"Tag told me to crash here," he stammers.

I nod, then bend to retrieve the evasive water bottle. Justin's palms cup my cheeks when I stand. In an instant his mouth crashes to mine.

"Mmm," I quietly protest.

His lips soften, gently massaging mine. While his speech is sloppy, his kiss is not. It's tender and hopeful. I push his large shoulders, breaking our connection. His heavy-lidded blue eyes attempt to focus on mine.

"Let's get you to bed," I suggest.

"That's exactly what I was thinking," he slurs with a smirk.

He stumbles often as I do my best to help him to the lower-level guest room. I'm grateful he plops hard to the mattress no longer interested in making out with me. Let's hope he has no recollection of the kiss by morning.

Remembering my quest for my phone, I set my course towards the pool house once again. I halt for a moment, hand on the French door handles. The pool lights are on, and Tag swims laps. *What are my chances of walking past him twice without him spotting me?* Excited to get my thoughts in my notes app, I take a deep breath before stepping from the house. At the far end of the pool, Tag touches the wall before his flip turn sends him towards me. My bare feet pad lightly on the warm pool deck. Out of the corner of my eye I watch him continue his lap. I breathe a sigh of relief when I enter the pool house.

The faint lights of the pool allow me to spot my cell phone on the kitchen island. I gently pull the pool house door closed behind me. Turning towards the main house, I find Tag hanging on the edge at the deep end of the pool, watching me.

"What are you doing?" he inquires.

I wave my cell phone between us. "I forgot where I left my phone," I answer. "Why can't you sleep?"

He shakes his head. In the pale lights I see his jaw clench.

"I didn't mean to interrupt," I explain and excuse myself.

Where once my thoughts were full of recipes, now concerns for Tag clog my thoughts. *How is he swimming laps if he drank as much as Justin? If he didn't drink that much, why did he let his friend? What thoughts haunt him tonight, causing him to paddle lap after lap? Why can't he take a break from laps one night with Justin here?*

I slip back under my sheet, careful not to wake Rachel. *What would he say... how would he react if I told him Justin kissed me tonight?* I brush away that thought. I don't intend to tell him, and I pray that Justin doesn't confess. Absent-mindedly, my fingertips brush over my lips as I remember the kiss. It wasn't a sloppy, drunk kiss. *If a drunk Justin's kiss is that good, imagine...* I scold myself. *I am not interested in Justin... or any guy.* While I don't long for a relationship now, it feels good to know I no longer fight the urge to puke at the touch of a man.

Needing to change my line of thought, I open my phone and begin making my list for my future videos.

14

TAG

Tuesday night, I lead my guests to the dining room. Bonnie set up the perfect table for our conversation with Justin at one end and me at the other. Standing at the head of the table, I notice Phoebe's name tent no longer labels the place setting nearest Justin, but she sits by me. I have no doubt, she rearranged it herself. Despite my constantly ignoring her, she still attempts to change our work relationship. *I need to tread carefully.*

When everyone takes a seat, I nod toward Bonnie in the corner to signal she may begin serving. Emma's friend Rachel joins her in filling water glasses and offering wine to our guests.

"This sounds delicious," Schuyler states, a small card in her hand.

It is not until she points it out that I notice the menu cards printed at each place setting. Apparently, Emma pulled out all the stops for my dinner this evening. I read:

Starter:
Scallops, spicy fennel, red wine marinara, toasted baguette

Entrée:
Frenched Lollipop Lamb Chop, sautéed spinach, blistered cherry tomato, garlic mashed potatoes, mint puree

Dessert:
Chocolate Dipped Strawberry Cheesecake

With each part of our meal, I am more impressed with Emma's wide culinary abilities. While Bonnie assured me she is capable of preparing a high quality meal for six, I worried this might be a challenge for her. All six plates arrive for each course on large trays at a perfect temperature for all of us. This is the type of service I expect from high-end caterers, not an eighteen-year-old, not-formally-trained, aspiring chef.

Between the bites of food followed by oohs and ahhs, Justin and I discuss our hopes and terms of investing in *Brink* restaurant and *Fringe,* the attached speakeasy Bar. Calvin and Garret agree with our terms, and by the time the dinner plates are cleared, we have a verbal agreement for Justin to begin the legal paperwork tomorrow to seal the deal.

Justin leans close as Bonnie lifts his empty plate. "You outdid yourself tonight," he compliments.

"This was not me," Bonnie informs, smiling widely, proud of Emma's handiwork.

"Did you hire a caterer?" my friend asks me across the table.

All eyes look toward me. I open my mouth to respond, but Pheobe beats me to it.

"I tried to hire a caterer," she grumbles, not pleased I put my trust in Emma.

Unwilling to allow Pheobe to pout out loud, I look to Bonnie. "Please ask Emma to join us."

When Emma enters the room, my chest swells at the sight of her in the new black chef's jacket I purchased for her with "Talk Foodie

To Me" under her name. Her hands cross nervously in front of her, and her cheeks pink with embarrassment.

"This is…" I begin to introduce her.

"Talk Foodie to Me!" the women cheer in unison.

"Emma, we watch every episode," Schuyler professes.

"Sometimes they even successfully recreate your recipes," Calvin teases.

"Be nice," Dallas chides. "Don't embarrass us."

"Our children request 'Memma's Tookies' all the time," Schuyler shares. "The kids helped me make your sugar cookies once and want them all the time."

Emma's cheeks morph from pink to red at their praise. "For dessert I prepared Chocolate Dipped Strawberry Cheesecake."

Rachel and Bonnie place one martini glass containing cheesecake with chocolate-dipped strawberries on top.

"Join us," Dallas encourages.

I send Pheobe to fetch a chair from the other room for Emma. When she returns, she shrewdly places it at Justin's end of the table. Over her antics, I urge Emma to sit next to me in Pheobe's chair.

Our group enjoys the first bites of Emma's dessert in silence.

Dallas points her fork in my direction. "I knew you looked familiar. You were in the cupcake episode this week."

Schuyler turns her attention towards Emma at my side. "Your new studio kitchen is fabulous."

"Want to see it?" Emma offers. Her wide eyes immediately fly to me. "I'm sorry. I do not want to interrupt…" She waves her hand around the table, signaling our business dinner.

"The business portion of our evening is complete. Justin will start our paperwork tomorrow," I inform her, ensuring she is not interrupting my business.

"Follow me to the pool house," Justin suggests, standing his dessert glass clean.

"Feel free to bring your desserts with you," I offer, following his lead.

The women inspect every part of the kitchen, appliances, and bakeware. They marvel at the cameras.

"We plan to make your cupcakes from your last video at our next Mommy & Me group," Schuyler states.

"Maybe we could arrange for your group to visit my kitchen," Emma offers. "If everyone is up for it, we could film an episode about cooking as a family."

They love Emma's idea and plan to contact her tomorrow to arrange it.

"I filmed tonight's dinner preparation," Emma states, much to the delight of the women. "Would the two of you like to film the ending with me?"

Squeals erupt. These adult women actually squeal with glee at the opportunity to appear on camera with Emma. The four of us laugh as the women require three takes before they are pleased with their salutation, waving and giggling into the camera. Emma lights up with the excitement and praise from our guests.

"The kids will flip when they see us in the next episode," Dallas exclaims.

This was the perfect finale to our business this evening. Emma urged me to consider finding a career I enjoyed within finance. She encouraged me to investigate venture capitalism. She created a masterpiece of a meal, and she provided the after-dinner entertainment.

Emma remains with Justin and I as we say goodnight to our guests. Calvin invites her to consider taking a chef position at their restaurant as they leave.

"So, Ems," Justin nudges her shoulder with his after I close the front door. "Ready to leave the waitress job for a chef position at Brink?"

Noticing lights still on, I stride toward the kitchen. I am prepared to do what I can to help Bonnie and Rachel clean-up for the night. However, over the muffled sounds of the dishwasher, Bonnie and

Rachel sit at the kitchen island. All surfaces show no sign of the large event held here tonight.

"What's up?" Rachel asks.

"I planned to help you with the clean-up," I admit, causing the women to giggle. "I should have known Bonnie had it all under control."

"The meal was a success. How did the business go?" Bonnie asks.

I smile warmly and nod. "I am officially a VC."

Bonnie claps while Rachel seems bored. I slip my hand inside my jacket pocket. I extend the white envelope towards Emma's friend.

"This is for you," I inform her. "Thank you for your help tonight."

Rachel's eyes grow wide, and her jaw drops at my gesture.

"I did this for Emma; I did not expect payment," she explains.

"I appreciate that. You helped Bonnie and me this evening. Buy yourself something fun," I encourage, shaking the envelope still in my hand.

She takes the proffered payment, clutching it tight to her chest. "Thank you," she beams, and I nod. "Emma, he paid me!"

Turning, I find the two girls huddled in conversation near the entrance to the kitchen.

"I'm exhausted," Bonnie announces. "I'll see you all in the morning." She stands, making her way to her quarters over the garage.

Justin and Rachel say goodnight, leaving Emma and I alone.

"Should we head to the pool house?" I ask, much to her surprise. "I will help you clean."

"You…" she stammers.

"I am not allowing you to clean up by yourself," I state.

"If you hired a caterer, they would do it without your help," she argues.

"Ahh, but you refused to allow me to pay you for your services this evening," I remind her of our ongoing argument for two days.

She relents, biting her lips as she turns to lead the way. To my dismay, Pheobe lingers nearby.

"That is all for tonight," I clip. "Take the day off tomorrow."

I do not wait for her reaction. Instead, a turn towards the French doors leading to the pool. "I really need to put more distance between us," I mumble, stepping outside.

"How do you share an office with her every day?" Emma asks, having heard my grumble.

Once the shock of being overheard clears I respond, "it is not conducive to work."

"The house is huge. Give her an office of her own," Emma suggests.

"She needs to be close by," I divulge.

"Then set up a reception desk outside your office. That area is quiet all day," she offers, pointing towards the French doors we recently stepped through as she walks backwards. "Put her back to the pool, and I should not distract her when I am out here."

I like this idea. Pheobe will hate it, but I think it will work.

Holding the pool house door open for Emma, I ask, "So, what did you think of Calvin and Garret's wives?"

"Why were they here tonight?" Emma counters, stacking dirty pots within each other next to the sink. "Are you bringing them on as new clients at the firm?"

I smile wide; she will love this. "They are my first investment in my new venture capitalist role," I divulge, leaning my forearms on a clear portion of the island opposite the sink.

I love her reaction. At first shock floods her face; then she smiles proud that I followed through on her suggestion that I find a career that I love within finance.

"Put me to work. How can I help?"

Emma scans the counters in all directions. Pointing to her left she asks me to place the spices in the cabinet door she opens beside the range. For my next task, she requests I place all utensils, bowls, and saucers into the dishwasher. She points at the stainless-steel dishwasher door, below the counter, as if I have no idea what it might look like. I fight the urge to spew a witty quip in my defense and set to my tasks.

"Since I listened to you about my career change," I smirk. "I think you should take your own advice. You love cooking. Anyone can see that." I pause, searching her face to see if I am overstepping my bounds and find Emma hanging on my every word. "I am not sure working at a restaurant makes you happy. You seem happier working in front of the camera, creating your video blog, and maybe working as a personal chef, like tonight, from time to time."

I work quietly to finish my task, allowing Emma time to consider my challenge for her. She finishes wiping down the counters while I flip off several lights throughout the space.

"Ready?" she asks, hand on the door.

I follow her back along the pool deck toward the main house.

"We should host a barbecue pool party," I suggest, looking at the dark pool water as we pass.

Emma stops in her tracks, turning to face me, eyebrows raised.

"I rarely use the space other than for swimming laps," I state. "It would be nice to utilize the space with our family and friends."

"So, Bonnie's family, Justin, and Rachel?" she seeks clarity on my statement.

"We could invite Calvin, Garret, and their families," I think out loud. "It could be a celebration of finalizing the paperwork this week."

"This week?" she squeaks.

"Friday," I announce. "If everyone is available, let's have a barbecue on Friday."

I love the idea of enlisting Emma's expertise to plan a casual pool party for this weekend. I long to keep her at my side as I start my new adventure.

Emma

"Grab a cart," I prompt as we enter Hy-Vee, my eyes scanning our shopping list one more time.

"Which kind?" Tag questions, confused.

I pry my eyes from our list on my cellphone to find Tag standing with one hand on the little shopping cart and one on the large one. I fight my giggle. We made the list together, so he knows how many items we need. I assumed this would be an uncommon experience for him, perhaps this is a first.

"Are you a grocery virgin?" I giggle, speaking low for only our ears.

He puckers his lips, nodding slightly. "I've been in a few liquor stores and gas stations," he chuckles.

Definitely a novice; this should be fun.

"Large shopping cart, please," I suggest. "We will start in the produce section." I point as I speak, showing him the area.

"How about I push the cart and you do all the shopping," he offers, hopeful. "I will simply watch and learn."

I agree because he is clearly out of his element here.

15

EMMA

For the umpteenth time today, I mentally list the food we planned and prepared along with the drinks and condiments to make sure we do not forget something. I pull my cell phone from my back pocket to check my list as Tag enters the kitchen.

"Taking a break?" Bonnie asks.

"I need to make two more phone calls, then I am off for the weekend," he announces proudly. "I think we forgot to plan desserts," Tag states, eyes bouncing from me to Bonnie and back.

"We have fresh fruit," I remind him.

Tag shakes his head. "I was thinking ice cream," he shares.

"I can run to the store for ice cream, cones, and toppings while you finish your work calls," I offer.

"I wanted to run something by you," he states, with a long pause. "Rolled ice cream."

Rolled ice cream? That is not something I can purchase when I swing by the local Hy-Vee store. I prepare to share this when he continues.

"A locally owned, rolled-ice cream company approached me, seeking an investment to purchase two more food trucks. If I call to see if they can swing their ice cream truck by here tonight, what time should I tell them?"

Look at him go. It is only a week since I mentioned changing his career to something he is passionate about, and he already has two prospects to invest in.

"Maybe seven," I suggest. "We could always stop what we are doing to eat ice cream."

"Sounds good," he beams, turns on his heels, and returns to his office.

Two hours later, Tag, Justin, and Drake surround the grill. The air fills with the smell of burgers and children enjoying the pool. Rachel and Bonnie assist me in carrying my homemade potato salad, my mom's famous baked beans, a relish tray, and condiments to the buffet table.

Calvin, the owner of the club *Fringe* sits on the edge of the pool with his wife, Schuyler, as their son and daughter splash in the water nearby. Two men own the restaurant and club; while one works tonight, the other spends the evening with us. Although her husband is working, the other owner's wife, Dallas, and their son swim. Tag's assistant, Pheobe camps on a lounge chair in an almost-inappropriate-to-wear-in-front-of-children red string bikini. I over-heard her apologize to Tag for not bringing a guest. Next to her, Rachel's sister lounges in her halter top and cut off jean shorts. Surprisingly everyone we invited is in attendance.

"Hot dogs are ready!" Justin calls over his shoulder, carrying a platter with a hotdog pyramid to the table.

The children cheer as they make their way to the pool steps and ladder, excited for dinner. Their parents scurry to wrap them in a towel and join them at the food table.

I approach the men at the grill.

"As soon as the cheese melts I will plate the burgers," Tag informs me.

"They smell divine," I gush, my stomach growling.

"What's the deal with your friend and her sister?" Drake asks, his eyes on Rachel sitting at the end of her sister's chair.

I look to Tag to decipher his friend's cryptic question. He rolls his eyes.

"Are they single or easily swayed to be single?" Drake continues his inquiry.

Oh, now I understand.

"Um, both are single… Well, last I heard Rachel's sister was still single," I share.

"Dibs on the older one," Drake calls, nudging Justin's shoulder.

"Easy there Casanova," Tag scolds. "There are children here."

I search Tag's face to see if he thinks Drake will seriously hit on my friends. His attention, however, is on sliding the burgers and brats from the grill to the platter. I do not know enough about Justin or Drake to know if I should warn my friends off or let them flirt.

Flip flops approaching, I turn to find my best friend.

"Yummy, yummy," Rachel croons, low near my ear.

I look out the side of my eye at her.

"Three hot guys and me, I like my odds," Rachel rejoices.

"Behave," I chide. "This is Tag's first get together. Don't bring drama and ruin it for him. He has clients here."

"Ye of little faith," she mocks.

Together we approach the line of guests at the buffet. The families with children sit around nearby patio tables, Bonnie and Barry hold plates in their laps in lawn chairs, as Pheobe and Rachel's sister fill their plates in front of us. Glancing over my shoulder, I find the men selecting beer from the cooler.

Tag seems relaxed in the company of his friends. *I like seeing him like this.* Over the past week, his designer suits and crisp tone faded into smiles and comfortable conversations.

"Emma, don't be rude," Drake chides. "Introduce us to your friend."

Beside me Rachel preens.

"Guys, this is Rachel," I introduce reluctantly. "Rachel, this is Justin and Drake."

"Can I get you a beer?" Drake offers, turning on his charm.

"She is only eighteen," Tag snarls in warning.

"We drank at eighteen," Drake counters. "Heck, we started drinking at…"

"Not in front of my other guests," Tag advises.

I swear I see Drake wink at my friend. *Oh brother, this may be a long night. Rachel eats up male attention.*

"I've seen you at the club, haven't I?" Drake asks. "You play tennis, right?"

Rachels beams, "Yes. Do you play?"

I nudge Rachel to fix her plate. With a paper plate in hand, I stand behind her. Following me, Justin smiles and nods.

"We should play some time," Rachel suggests. "Maybe we could drag Tag and Emma along."

Tag

"Emma plays tennis?" I blurt like an idiot.

We live under the same roof and belong to the same club. I should know whether or not she plays tennis and golf.

"Tag, these burgers are sublime," Pheobe gushes from her lounge chair.

I smile in her direction. It pleases me to see she opted for a cover up. It is open down the front and lacy, but it does cover up a bit more of her skin than the red bikini. I prefer not to see my employee nearly naked at my pool.

"Hey," I call for only Justin and Drake to hear. "Red bikini is off limits."

Justin nods his understanding, while Drake's eyes lock on Pheobe.

"She is my assistant and absolutely not available," I warn.

"Not available? Or off limits?" Drake seeks clarification.

"Does not matter," Justin states. "Tag says she is an employee and off limits, so don't mess with her."

"Got it," Drake reluctantly agrees. "What about Rachel and Emma?"

"Dude," Justin admonishes. "Emma is Tag's stepsister, so extremely off limits."

"She is not my stepsister," I correct in a growl. "She's my step-niece."

"So she is back in play," Drake hopes.

I open my mouth to warn him off Emma once and for all, but rein in my sudden rage.

"Emma is off limits," Justin declares a little louder than I like. "Tag didn't invite us here to hook up. Act your age."

I close my eyes, drawing breath through my nose. I fan my face with my paper plate, attempting to erase this entire conversation and the feelings it stirs in me. When I open my eyes, Drake, with his full plate, approaches the empty chair near Rachel's sister and Pheobe. Justin stands at the end of the long table, squirting mustard on his hamburger bun. I turn, scanning the patio and pool deck. My makeshift family, friends, and colleagues litter the area, enjoying food and conversation. *I like this.*

My eyes look to Emma, sitting on the diving board beside Rachel with her plate in her lap. When I catch her looking at me; she quickly turns her eyes down to the food in her lap.

I wonder what she is thinking?

Emma

"Yes!" Drake cheers, high-fiving Tag.

I duck out of their way and wade through the water to the other side of the volleyball net to shake the hands of Rachel and Justin. Our team won three of the four games of water volleyball we play after ice cream and the families with children left. I climb the ladder, snagging a towel from a nearby table. Tag joins me as I dry off.

"Should I say something?" he asks, his voice low.

I follow the direction of his gaze to Rachel and Justin wrestling in the pool. Justin's arms hug Rachel's back tight to his chest as he dunks the two of them over and over under the water. During the volleyball games, I observed the two bump into each other a few times, high five each other, and flirt constantly. I made a mental note to ask Tag about Justin later. His pointing them out now, causes me more concern.

"Should I worry about Justin with my friend?" I murmur, towel drying my hair.

"I want to ask the same thing about Rachel," he chuckles deeply.

"She likes to flirt, but she means well," I share. "Is he a player, an ass, or a dawg?"

Tag's hand freezes, pressing a towel to the back of his neck. His brow furrows and eyes squint.

"He is a great guy. Perhaps he trusts too easily," Tag shares.

I nod before pulling my t-shirt over my head.

"Tag," Pheobe coos. "Might I use the shower in the pool house? I need to wash off all the sunscreen."

Now standing beside us, she slowly drags her index finger from her shoulder toward her navel. I sneak a glance out the corner of my eye. I am surprised to find Tag looks towards Drake at the beer cooler instead of following her fingers to her cleavage as she intended.

"Taagg," she drawls.

"Go ahead," he answers, lifting his chin when Drake holds up a beer.

I fight a chuckle at Pheobe's little huff before walking in the direction of the pool house. Completely ignoring her, Tag lowers himself into a nearby patio chair.

"I am ready for her to leave," he grumbles, low enough I wonder if I imagined it.

He taps my leg with his towel.

"Are you having fun?" he juts his chin towards our friends in the pool.

I smile and nod.

"Are you?" I throw his question back to him.

"I closed my second business deal tonight," he informs, proudly.

"I assume you are officially in the restaurant, club, and rolled ice cream business now," I surmise.

"Verbally, yes. Ice cream is not final until paperwork is signed in the next week or two," he elaborates.

"Congr…"

"Not yet," he interrupts. "Don't jinx it. We can celebrate when it is final."

"Celebrate what?" Justin asks from the edge of he pool.

"Nothing yet," Tag tells him, while giving me a look, encouraging me not to share any details.

"What's going on in there?" Drake asks, handing Tag his beer and motioning toward the pool house.

All eyes swing in that direction as Pheobe walks by the large windows, wearing nothing but a small green towel. She walks from one side of the house to the other and back, providing twice the opportunity for the guys to spot her. In my gut I feel this is all part of her plan to dig her claws into Tag.

I wonder what Tag thinks about this?

16

EMMA

"Don't you think Tag resembles Hunter Hayes with his hair wet?"
Rachel murmurs low from the edge of the pool beside me.

My face pinches while I think. *Do I know what Hunter Hayes looks like?*
Rachel leans her cell phone in front of me, Pinterest pictures on
display. *Hmm.* I peek over the top of Rachel's cell phone at a laugh-
ing, dripping wet Tag in the center of the pool. *Who knew Tag could be
messy? Who knew messy Tag could look so... hot?*

Tag

Rachel wades through the water, approaching Emma at the side of
the pool, mere feet from me. I cannot hear the conversation, but my
eyes locked on Emma's face. I watch disbelief morph as Emma
attempts to pull herself together before speaking. I know she is not

happy with Rachel, but she attempts to act as if she is. I approach when Rachel swims excitedly towards Justin.

Emma stares at her ankles and feet kicking softly in the water as I approach.

"Hey," I greet nervously, sidling to the edge of the pool beside her.

The warm sunlight pushes the cool water from my abdomen as I stand in the shallow end of the pool. I do not hear Emma respond. Several nervous moments pass while we watch our friends in the pool.

"Everything okay?" I ask, hoping she will open up to me.

Emma nods. Out of the corner of my eye, I see Bonnie wave me to come to her. I place my hand on Emma's knee, letting her know I will be right back.

Trudging through the water, I make my way towards the sunken steps at the shallowest section of our pool. A smile slides upon my face as I step closer to my mother figure.

"I need to ask a favor of you," she murmurs low and serious.

The answer will be yes. I will do everything in my power to help this woman for the rest of my life.

"Emma's friend just bailed on her for the entire weekend," Bonnie informs me. "I'm not asking you to devote your entire weekend to her; maybe hang out with her tonight?"

Worry coats Bonnie's features. She knows I try to appease her any time she needs it. In offering to pay for Kate's college and moving her family to live in my house, I preempted her needs. She is like a mother to me; like a good son, I strive to keep her happy. Keeping Emma company tonight will not be a burden. She helped me with the barbecue; I look forward to paying her back.

I saunter over to the lounge chairs near Emma. I take a seat at the foot of one.

"I cannot thank you enough for helping me pull this off," I tell her.

She looks from her friend leaving with mine to where I sit. A slow, sweet smile slips upon her face, and her warm eyes heat my heart.

"I enjoyed every minute of it," she claims.

"Let's clean up. Then crawl into comfortable clothes and crash," I suggest.

"I hear a bath and a book calling my name," Emma claims.

In her voice I hear her disappointment in Rachel bailing on her this evening. She will not admit it to me, so I will pretend I know nothing.

"Do you have plans for tonight?" I prod.

Emma shakes her head, "Bubbles and a book."

"Justin and I were going out," I share. "But he bailed."

She cringes at my mention of going out.

"I am not in the mood to go anyway, but I might be up for a movie or two," I propose, hoping she will take the bait. "Comfy clothes in the theater room sound good to you?"

Emma's eyes search mine.

"You can pick the first movie," I offer hopefully.

"Really?" Her eyes grow wide with excitement.

I nod. "I get to pick the second movie."

"As long as you don't choose a horror movie," she counters, and I nod in agreement. "Deal," she giggles, hopping over to pick up beach towels and tossing them into the nearby bin. "I was supposed to watch movies with Rachel tonight," she admits while working.

I strum up all my remaining energy to clear the pool deck and to help Bonnie and Emma in the kitchen.

"Scram!" Bonnie orders, pointing to the two of us through the kitchen door. "I can finish."

The counters clean, the two dishwashers running, and the leftovers in the refrigerator, I feel there is not much left for Bonnie to do on her own.

17

TAG

Each in a comfy shirt and shorts, Emma and I meet in the theater.

"What is our first movie?" I ask, descending the stairs.

She thinks about it for a couple of steps. Entering the hallway, she turns to walk backward, a huge smile upon her face. "Anything I want to watch?" Emma asks, and I nod.

"You cue up a movie; I will make the popcorn."

Emma stops in her tracks at the door to the media room. "Really?"

I chuckle. "We can't have a movie night without popcorn," I state. "You planned to eat popcorn with Rachel, didn't you?"

"I love popcorn," she grins, clapping.

My insides warm with the knowledge I elicited that reaction from her. It surprises me that it pleases me to please her. I have an overwhelming desire to make her happy; part of me wants to make it my goal every day from here forward.

As the popcorn machine spins, slowly heating the kernels in the oil, I watch Emma carry two large pillows and two throw blankets in from the hallway, tossing them into recliners in the front row. While the kernels pop loudly, she pulls two water bottles from the mini fridge, placing them in nearby cup holders. Pulling my attention from her, I scramble to ready two containers and not burn the popcorn.

"I love the smell of popcorn," Emma purrs when I pass her a bowl then set mine on the armrest.

"Need anything else before we start?" I ask, positioning my pillow on the far side of my seat and tossing the blanket into the chair beside mine.

Emma places her pillow on her far armrest and pulls a blanket over her. She settles her steaming hot bowl of popcorn into her lap. Taking the remote in hand, I press play, starting our movie.

Of course, she chose a chick flick. I should have predicted a rom-com was in my future the minute I allowed her to choose.

"Have you seen this movie?" Emma inquires, pausing our movie when the title, *How To Lose A Guy In 10 Days*, appears on the screen.

"I think so," I lie.

"My favorite part is when she brings him the love fern," she informs. "Or when Matthew McConaughey says, 'Krull the warrior king,'" she recites in a growling voice, cracking herself up.

"Press play, you dork," I laugh with her.

Fifteen minutes into the movie, and I rethink my second movie choice. I long to find another one that she will laugh and quote adorably beside me.

The credits roll; I scoop up the empty popcorn bowls and water bottles, carrying them to the kitchenette in the back of the room. Emma remains curled up under her blanket, leaning against the large pillow.

"I learned a lot about you this week," I announce with a smirk.

Rising, Emma quirks a brow, elbows on her hips. "Like?"

"I heard you play tennis and golf, you like to watch football, you are a Hawkeye fan, and you volunteer at the dog shelter." *I hope I do not come off as a stalker by listening to her conversations.*

One word describes Emma's facial expression: whoa. I fear I over shared. *Maybe I should have listed two items instead of five.* I return to the front of the theater.

"I must confess I am surprised you wanted to spend time with me this evening," she confesses. "I had the feeling you detest everything about me."

Wow! If I did not know better, I would believe alcohol brought on her honesty. My eyes now open to the error of my ways for three years; I need to apologize. She needs to know it was more about me than her.

"What do you remember about my mother?" I inquire.

Emma's face pinches, and her eyes narrow. She does not speak.

"I am very aware of what my mother was like. You will not offend me with your honesty," I offer.

"As a little girl, I liked to run into my grandfather's arms or hop onto his lap when I came over," she shares. "Elaine frowned upon my childish behavior. I overheard your mother tell grandfather that he should not condone my running in the house, sitting on his lap, and raising my voice."

I nod my head. "Even before she met Frank, mother expected perfection from me," I share. "In elementary school, I was always too heavy for her liking. Once puberty hit, I became too skinny. She hired a nutritionist to help me lose weight and later to pack on the pounds. My hair was too long and then too short. She detested my natural dirty-blonde strands and paid for highlights from the time I turned ten. In fifth grade, mother conveniently planned trips during my winter and spring breaks, forcing me to remain at school. I remember on one phone call, homesick, I begged to travel with her or stay home with Bonnie. Mother stated I could wait until May, by then my braces would be off and I could visit."

Emma's jaw drops. A silent moment passes as she attempts to process my mother's parenting style.

"Subconsciously, I believe I was jealous of your freedoms and cast expectations on you like my mother placed on me," I offer as explanation. "I worked hard to be taken seriously at the firm, as well as in the community, and I feared all would fade away with one wrong move."

I run my hands down my face, drawing in a long breath. "I am sorry for my abysmal behavior the past three years. Spending time with you recently, I regret the years I wasted avoiding you."

Emma places her hand upon my forearm and gently squeezes.

"I've enjoyed spending time with you this week," she murmurs with a sweet smile. "In fact, the more you smile, the more I want to be around you."

"I have never smiled as much as I have this week," I state. "Your challenge for me to consider a career shift sparked it all. I cannot thank you enough for your honesty and caring enough to notice my dissatisfaction. You saw beyond my façade."

Still smiling, she shrugs. "That's what family does," she makes light of the fact she helped me.

My head tilts, and my eyes narrow at her words. "It might sound strange; I never thought of you as my niece."

Emma's tongue darts out and swipes between her lips before her lips disappear between her teeth.

"Do I feel like your uncle?" I challenge, longing to understand how she sees the relationship between us.

Emma chuckles, confusing me. *Perhaps this proved to be too much honesty on my part.*

"Rachel and I attended the Iowa versus Iowa State games your Junior and Senior year," she informs me of something I did not know. "Our seats in your junior year at Jack Trice Stadium were amid season ticket holders. Rachel shared with the adults around us that I was related to the Iowa quarterback. When she attempted to explain that you were my step-uncle, the nearby crowd doubted that to be true. One of them explained that you were too close to my age and not married to my aunt or uncle, so you shouldn't be labeled a step-uncle. The consensus was that we weren't raised as relatives and you might be closer to a step-sibling than a step-uncle." She draws in a quick breath. "From that game on, I no longer considered you a family member. And I quit even mentioning how I knew you."

Okay? Not her step-uncle and not a step-sibling. Friends? I guess she thinks of us more as friends. I can work with that. And she attended two of my college games—I had no idea.

"What will our second movie be?" she inquires, apparently done with this conversation.

"Honestly, I rarely watch movies, so I have no idea what to select," I hedge.

"Trust me to choose another?" she asks, chewing on her lower lip.

"Of course," I reply, caring not one bit what we watch.

"Then *Pitch Perfect* it will be," she announces, picking up the remote with a yawn. "I'm sort of tired," she confesses.

"If you fall asleep, I will find a permanent marker and draw on your face," I warn, remembering an episode of *Friends* I watched with my mother when I was young, where Ross and Rachel doodled on each other's faces.

"You wouldn't," she scoffs.

I nod, beaming proudly at her reaction to my humor.

"Fall asleep and find out," I challenge.

I could care less if I finish the second movie, but I do not want to move and disturb Emma as she sleeps with her head resting on my shoulder.

So tired, she snores lightly. I contemplate laying her down in the recliner or carrying her to bed. *What would a friend do? What would a gentleman do?* I long to lie beside her, my arms around her for the night, but decide the opposite is the appropriate thing to do.

I slip from beneath her head, scooping her up wedding-night style to carry her upstairs. I notice movement in the kitchen as I approach the second stairway. I hoped to slip by without Bonnie noticing, but halfway up I see Bonnie standing in the doorway, light of the kitchen behind her, eyes watching me.

I slowly step into Emma's bedroom, feeling like I am intruding upon her personal space. *How do I pull the covers back and lay her down, without disturbing her?*

"You can put me down," Emma's sleepy voice surprises me. "I can walk."

Focused on transitioning her to bed, I neglected to see her wake.

When she wiggles, I release her legs, and she slides down my body to stand. Not ready to let her go, my hands remain on her hips. Our bodies press together from our waist to our knees. Emma looks up to me through her dark lashes.

On their own, my lips lower. My eyes locked on hers, I press my mouth upon her soft lips. My heart skips a beat when her eyes close and she does not pull away. Our mouths meld together. I press gently; she commits to the kiss. Opening and closing my lips over hers, I draw our interaction out.

When she pulls away, I struggle to breathe. My eyes search hers.

"Good night," she whispers, palms on my pecs pushing me toward her bedroom door.

I walk on clouds to my bedroom on the other side of the house. My thoughts remain on Emma as I climb into bed.

I did not imagine it, she kissed me back. My mind replays the slow, sensual interaction. I never experienced a kiss so sweet.

I toss and turn trying to wind down. I did not see it coming, but now all I want to do is repeat it. My mind and heart reel from our one soft, slow kiss. I am already addicted to everything about her. One sweet kiss sparks overwhelming emotion and ignites lust within me.

Emma

I stare at my ceiling, my fingertips gliding over my lips. The memory of his mouth on mine is fresh in my mind. I felt everything in his kiss. Our bodies close, our hands did not wander. I found hope and tenderness, as well as lust in his sweet kiss.

I didn't see it coming, but I didn't freeze in shock. Instead, my body immediately engaged with him. For once my heart led instead of my head.

He kissed me. My fingertips freeze upon my lower lip.

He kissed me. He. Kissed. Me. Tag, my step-uncle, kissed me!

I can't breathe; the air in my room grows stale and bile climbs my throat. *It's wrong—very wrong. We are related. Aren't we? I mean he isn't my blood relative, but legally he is my step-uncle. Legally?* Our conversation from earlier tonight replays in my head. *We don't feel like relatives, but to everyone we are.*

What once was a sweet moment between us now scares me. *Did I cause it? Did I lead him on in any way? It must be wrong. We can't. It can never happen again.*

Hot tears trickle down my cheek to my neck.

18

TAG

"Good morning," I announce, entering the kitchen. "What have you created for breakfast this fine morning?" I do not try to hide my good mood.

"Well, good morning to you," Bonnie greets amid her jolly laughter. "I have your favorite southwestern egg white omelet, bacon, toast, and fresh-squeezed orange juice."

I take my usual seat at the kitchen island, hopeful that Emma joins us. Bonnie makes quick work of the omelet as she slides a juice glass and toast on a saucer in front of me.

"I'm glad you watched movies with Emma last night," she shares. "She seemed disappointed that Rachel skipped out on her."

"I forgot to bring the popcorn bowls up," I state, shaking my head. I meant to go back down for them after I carried Emma to bed.

"I've already been down there."

I should have known; Bonnie is always on top of things. It is why I meant to bring them up last night. She does so much for us, the least I could do is lighten her load a bit.

"It does my heart good to see the two of you getting along," she says, placing my omelet in front of me. Her hand on top of mine, she

76

adds, "I've often thought the two of you would hit it off if you could spend a little time together."

"She is funny," I state.

Bonnie nods. "You could use a little humor in your life."

I wink at her, causing her to balk. Laughter bursts from my chest at her reaction.

I pause eating. "Do you have a minute?"

"For you, always," she answers. "Let me dry my hands."

I watch as she pulls her hands from the dishwater, drying them on the kitchen towel she keeps over her right shoulder. Once she places the towel back on her shoulder, her eyes look to mine.

"I did something," I confess, tearing the bandage off. "Well, we did something, and I need an unbiased opinion."

Bonnie squints her eyes as she reads my face.

"Emma and I enjoyed watching movies last night," I begin, and a wide smile forms on her face. "Well, it was totally unplanned, but it happened, and I'm glad it did." I look to her for input.

Bonnie remains on the other side of the countertop, leaning her back against the cabinets lining the wall. A long silence passes between us.

"Tag, you mentioned something happened, but you did not tell me what *it* was," she informs through her laugh.

I run my words through my head and find she is right.

"I kissed Emma when I carried her to bed last night," I confess.

Bonnie's face gives no hint to her reaction.

"It caught her off guard," I state.

"I am sure it did. The two of you only recently started *tolerating* one another," she shares what I know. "Did Emma... kiss you back?"

I nod with a smirk. "Yes. I need to know what to do now."

"Well," Bonnie draws out. "Hmm..."

I sense there is more to her deliberation than I know.

"Emma didn't pull away?" she inquires.

"She definitely kissed me back," I brag, fighting a smirk.

"What did she do after the kiss," Bonnie asks with a furrowed brow.

"We stood looking at each other for a second," I recall. "She whispered, 'Good night,' Then softly pushed my chest."

Long moments pass; I search Bonnie's face. The longer she is silent, the more worried I become.

"So, she didn't slap you, shove you, or cry?" Bonnie scrutinizes, and I shake my head.

What makes Bonnie think that Emma might have slapped me or cried?

"Hmm... You need to wait. Wait for her to bring it up."

Not the news I wanted to hear. Bonnie's wisdom served me well in the past. *It will not be easy, but I will comply.*

"I am going to spend the afternoon with her if she will let me," I announce.

"Don't push her if she turns you down. She might need time to process spending the evening with you that ended in a kiss," Bonnie advises.

"Do me a favor," I encourage. "If she brings it up, put in a good word for me. We opened up about the past, and I apologized for my actions. I think she saw my sincerity. I hope she did; I like spending time in her presence."

Bonnie's smile returns, and I wink at her.

"You know I will," she beams. "Remember Emma's younger and might need time to process your new friendship... and the kiss."

19

EMMA

I notice movement out the corner of my eye on my way to the kitchen. I pause to take in the scene. Tag sits at the patio table, laptop open, and phone to his ear. *That is odd.*

"Good morning," I greet on my way into the kitchen.

Bonnie turns from the stovetop, smiling in my direction before she places my coffee mug on the center of the island. As I take my first sip, I watch her remove a red bowl from the refrigerator. I balk when she slides the bowl in front of me.

Peering into the bowl, I find yogurt topped with fresh sliced strawberries, bananas, and blueberries. I look up to find Bonnie offering me granola to sprinkle on top. Frozen in place, I can only stare in disbelief.

"What's this?" I whisper.

Bonnie smiles and shrugs, "He asked me to give it to you."

"He? Like Tag he?" I scoff.

At her nod, I take the bowl and my coffee in hand, making my way to the pool deck. At the sound of the door closing behind me, Tag's head turns in my direction. He lifts his chin, holding up one finger, gesturing for me to wait a moment.

Not especially excited to discuss the awkwardness of our kiss, I turn back toward the house. To my horror I hear him wrap up his call and trot after me.

"Hey, what are your plans for the day?" Tag asks, hand on my shoulder, as I step into the kitchen.

I turn to face him, raising one eyebrow.

"I cleared my schedule. I thought maybe we could hang out," he shares, hopeful.

I climb onto a kitchen stool.

Caught off guard by this entire interaction, I play with the spoon pushing around the yogurt.

"Rachel and I planned to layout by the pool, shop a bit, order pizza, and watch more movies," I grumble, eyes on the spoon. "I texted and called, but she won't answer me." I can't hide the worry in my voice and in my expression. "It's not like her to ignore me. Normally, she would be faunching at the bit to share everything that happened with Justin last night." I chuckle, hollowly. "She tends to overshare."

Tag's thumbs fly on his cell phone screen.

Tag

I text my buddy.

> ME
>
> Emma is freaking out
>
> have Rachel reply to her texts
>
> NOW!

> JUSTIN
>
> (thumbs up emoji)

A minute later, Emma's cell phone rings in her pocket. While she answers, Bonnie sneaks me a thumbs up for solving this problem for Emma. I hang around, waiting for her answer to my question about her plans for the day.

Emma

"How was your movie night?" Bonnie asks me.

"We had fun." I nervously look to Tag, the terror of the inappropriate kiss on my mind.

"The popcorn was phenomenal if I do say so myself," Tag laughs.

"Who made the popcorn?" Bonnie inquires.

"I did," Tag claims proudly.

"Who picked the movie that Emma fell asleep to?" she asks.

I point to Tag and he lowers his head in faux shame. He does not inform Bonnie that he let me pick the second movie.

"In his defense, I was very sleepy by the end of my movie," I rescue.

Bonnie grins. "I love this." She points from me to Tag and back with the utensil in hand.

This? There is no this. Did Tag tell her we kissed? Surely not. She would be lecturing each of us if she knew we kissed.

"I need to make two more calls," Tag claims. "Let me know if you can hang out today."

Damn Rachel for bailing on me.

I watch Tag's back as he heads back toward his office. I'm glad he has other calls to make. I am not sure how to act around him this morning. Thoughts of our kiss last night still haunt me. *What was he thinking? How did that happen between the two of us?* Society sees him as my step-uncle, and I need to ensure we never make that mistake again.

"What's got you all bound up this morning?" Bonnie asks, pointing her wooden spoon in my direction.

"Nothing," I lie.

"Don't give me that," she admonishes. "You're in your head. What's going on?"

I want to brush her off, but the years have taught me she will not let up. She's like a dog with a bone.

"It sounds like the two of you had fun last night," Bonnie continues, seeking a reason for my distant thoughts.

"We did," I agree.

"So, what happened? Did he say something this morning?"

I shake my head. "It's just weird. I mean… he is my step-uncle. Hanging out with him is just plain weird."

She places her hands upon her rotund hips, spoon still in one hand. "Phish. The two of you are close in age, you have much in common… I love that you are becoming close."

"And that is not weird to you?" I ask.

Bonnie shrugs. "He's not really your uncle. With the little time the two of you have ever spent together, it's as if you were never in the same family."

I arch my brow.

"What I'm saying is, he is not your uncle. You are two people getting to know each other—nothing more," she explains her logic.

"But he's my guardian," I argue.

"On paper, yes," she agrees. "But you know as well as I do that he never acted as your guardian. He left that to me—not that I am complaining."

I nod. She's right. But on paper he is my step-uncle and guardian.

"I can count on one hand the people that know anything about Tag in your life," she continues her debate. "And even they know the line between the two of you was thin as a thread."

Is she right? I wish Rachel wasn't so caught up in lust for Justin. I could really use another opinion on this topic.

"Don't let yourself get too caught up in worries. I think the two of you should keep getting to know one another," Bonnie urges, sincerity heavy in her tone. "The two of you need each other. Trust me, you are perfect for each other."

Wait! What? She means as friends... right? She must mean we need each other as friends. She can't be insinuating we become something more. Yep. She wants us to be friends — that's all.

20

TAG

I did not think I could enjoy a day lounging by the pool without Justin, alcohol, and several women in tiny bikinis, but the afternoon hours fly by with Emma. We swim and float on rafts.

Frustrated, Emma tosses her cell phone on the end of the lounger when I return from the pool house restroom. I join her, sitting at the edge of the pool. Her good mood disappeared during my absence.

As we sit at the pool's edge, our feet in the water, Emma bites the corner of her lower lip, and her eyes focus on mine. I bump my shoulder to hers, urging her to open up.

"I'm worried about Rachel," she mumbles.

"Is she ignoring you again?"

Emma slowly kicks her feet in the water. "Still," she answers, her voice tense. "She tends to jump in headfirst, and I am afraid spending a night in Omaha will encourage her. What kind of guy is Justin?"

She turns her head toward me, eyes imploring me to be honest.

"He is a good guy," I promise.

"The kind of 'good guy'," she makes air quotes. "That kissed me last weekend then takes my best friend to Omaha this weekend?" She challenges.

"What?" I do not believe she said that.

"Um-hmm," she assures me I did indeed hear her correctly. "He was drunk, but I did not imagine the kiss."

What the hell? Justin would not do this. It is bro-code, and as my best friend, Emma is off limits. *He wouldn't. Last weekend. Last weekend.* Emma's birthday party was last Saturday night. We shared drinks with Kate before we left the group to hang out on our own. He did drink more than normal and...

Justin was in a sentimental mood. He brought up his ex and his inability to find a girl like Kate, Rachel, and Emma. His thoughts combined with alcohol, made for a boring conversation. I suggested he stay instead of drive home. When he went to the guest room, I swam laps.

"Justin kissed you?"

Emma nods. "He was clunking around the kitchen when I went to fetch my phone. I helped him grab a water, and..."

"He kissed you?"

"Yes," she chuckles. "Justin kissed me. He was drunk, and I had to help him back to his room."

I am dumbfounded.

"So... is Justin a dawg? Will I be spending my week with Rachel crying on my shoulder?" Eyebrows raised, Emma demands my honesty.

"Justin is a good guy," I repeat. "He is not a player. He does not sleep with a new girl every week. He is actually searching for the perfect woman to settle down with," I scoff.

My words seem to calm her nerves. If only they calmed my anger that my best friend kissed Emma.

"Why aren't you engaged?" she blurts.

I splash water on her.

She laughs as she dabs her face with a nearby towel.

What brought that on? Was it our kiss last night? Has she been thinking about it all day like I have?

"I mean..." she stammers. "This is a large house; you should be searching for a wife to fill it with children."

Whoa! I did not see this conversation turn.

"As your...um... step-niece," her eyes move back and forth between mine, unsure how to continue. "It's my duty to make sure you are happy."

"And you believe a wife and kids would make me happy?" I inquire.

"I see you with several kids," she states. "Running from sports and other activities, swimming in the backyard, holding family cookouts... Something about you screams 'family man'."

"I am not really interested in a wife right now," I confess. "I am rather busy changing my career path, as you suggested last week."

"Dating would not interfere with work," she argues. "It might even be a stress reliever and take your mind off business for a bit. Once or twice a week couldn't hurt."

Is she serious? What about me gives her the impression I am the "settle down and start a family" type of guy?

"Are you dating?" I blurt, attempting to escape the hot seat she placed me in.

"Uh-uh," she smiles, shaking her head. "No changing the subject, I asked you first."

Her sweet face and light blue eyes urge me to speak honestly. *How did I ignore this earnest woman for three years?*

"I date occasionally," I inform her.

"I never saw you bring a date home," Emma states. "A one night stand is not dating."

"That's..."

"That is an honest observation," she claims.

I want to lie and claim I see a woman more than one night, but for the most part I do not. I stare at my hands as I ponder. I have a steady hookup that is nothing more than a booty call. I like my freedom. I had a girlfriend in high school for four months. That proved to be the most brutal four months of my life. My days consisted of drama and fighting; we spent our nights making up. She asked me to account for my whereabouts when not in her presence, and pouted when I planned to spend time with my friends and teammates. The real drama ensued when a female spoke to me or even looked in my direction. I do not care to return to that type of relationship.

"I can't seem to find the right woman to make me want to spend time with her," I admit.

Hesitantly, I glance up at Emma through my lashes.

"Maybe we should find you a new place to look for women," she suggests.

"Where do you meet guys?" I inquire, placing her on the hot seat with me.

She shakes her head. I assume she plans to chastise me for attempting to change the subject once more, but it seems she avoids my question. Long moments of silence fall between us.

"Emma." My voice expresses my concern.

"Guys aren't interested in me," she murmurs before rising and making her way to the nearest lounge chair. She dries her calves and feet.

Bullshit. It was not that long ago that I attended high school. She is gorgeous, smart, and creative… any guy would be lucky to be with her.

I take a seat on the chair beside hers.

"I call bullshit," I protest.

She sneers.

"Bonnie mentioned you attending dances in high school," I inform her.

"I've dated," she admits, barely above a whisper.

"Are you seeing anyone now?"

What prompted me to ask that? I watch Emma struggle with her answer.

"Like you said, I haven't found someone special enough to spend more time with." She lets out a loud sigh. "Since I am not into casual dating or casual… uh… you know. Kate suggested I look into an app or online dating," she shares, her vulnerable blue eyes begging me not to make fun of her.

I cannot stand her discomfort. Although I did not start this conversation, I decide to end it.

"Maybe…"

"Maybe what?" I ask, leaning towards her.

"We could help each other create a profile," she suggests.

Emma avoids eye contact after her comment.

"I am not sure I am the kind of guy to use…"

She interrupts me, "I will do it if you will."

"I will help you create yours," I offer.

"How about this, I create a profile for you, and you create mine. Then we will choose one match for each other to go on a date with," she proposes.

I shake my head.

"Are you scared?" she taunts.

"No," I scoff.

"Then we'll do it," she states with a wide smile and a nod.

"Are you serious?" I chuckle, disbelieving.

"Yes," she immediately answers. "Go get your laptop; I'll grab mine. We can create the profiles before we eat dinner."

I do not budge.

"Hurry," she urges. "Bonnie said dinner will be ready in an hour. Let's meet in your office."

Emma quickly secures a towel around her waist and slips on her flip flops. I follow her from the pool area. While she climbs the stairs to her room, I wake my laptop on my desk. *How in the world did she talk me into this?*

21

TAG

Across from me, Emma's fingers fly over her keyboard.

"What is your biggest pet peeve?" She asks me.

"That's a hard one," I mumble.

I take my time considering my answer. *Pet peeve. Pet peeve. Hmm.*

Emma's warm eyes await my response. She really is a beautiful girl with her flawless skin, pert nose, and full pink lips.

"Tag," she prompts, drawing my thoughts back to the question.

"Reality TV shows," I blurt and wish I had come up with a better answer.

"Really?" Emma scoffs.

"Your turn," I prompt, even though I am not at that part of the profile yet.

"Empty coffee cups," she answers.

I scoff, "That is not a pet peeve."

"Yes, it is," she argues. "I hate when I watch TV or a movie and the actor has a paper coffee cup in their hand with or without a lid."

She looks to me for understanding.

"They hold the cup unnaturally," she explains "And when they sit it on the table it sounds empty. I mean, how hard is it to put a little water in the cup? That way they would hold it like it had coffee in it, and it would not sound empty when they set it down."

"Wow."

"Wow what?" she asks.

"You pay way more attention when you watch than I do," I chuckle.

Emma shrugs, then challenges, "Pay attention next time, you'll see what I mean."

My eyes squint a bit as I study her. She is not pulling my chain; she is serious. This is her pet peeve. She turns her gaze from me toward her screen, and I return to filling out her dating profile.

"Are you seeking a man, a woman…"

"A man," she giggles.

"Picky about the age?" I ask.

Emma looks toward the ceiling for a moment.

"Between 18 and 30," she answers.

Thirty? Interesting. I imagined she would use twenty-two or twenty-three as her upper limit. The thought of Emma at age eighteen seeing a thirty-year-old man leaves a bad taste in my mouth.

"What age range did you choose for me?" I wonder out loud.

"Don't you worry," she giggles, returning to her laptop. "I know exactly what to select to find you a date."

"We will see about that," I hedge. "Preference on smoking?"

Emma sticks out her tongue and mimics gagging.

"I will take that as a hard limit," I chuckle and type. "Your favorite place to hang out is… the kitchen."

Emma pulls her lips between her teeth, fighting a smile.

"What book are you reading?" I ask.

"I'm reading *Ali's Fight* by Brooklyn Bailey," she grins.

I make a mental note to investigate that book. I suddenly have the urge to read it. I should ask what she posted for me, but I expect she will tell me to trust her again. *How did I get myself into this?* The last thing I want to do is go on a date with a woman she finds online. I might act like I am going along with this, but I plan to pretend to go on a date.

"Done!" I announce.

On Emma's computer screen I see she is already scrolling through matches. *Yikes. She is really all-in on her task.*

I slowly start viewing matches for Emma. *No. No. No. Hell no!* The first five matches are all older than twenty-five. I don't see her with a guy six or more years older than her.

"When should we plan this date for?" Emma asks, her laptop screen now turned away from me. "How does Friday sound?"

"Friday, as in days from now?" I sputter.

Is she serious? Does she want to hurry this along for my benefit, or is she lonely and serious about finding a guy?

"This was your idea; you choose," I state, dreading this more and more by the minute.

"Friday it is then," Emma declares.

Why do I want to do this to make her happy?

"Dinner's ready," Bonnie announces with a quick knock, peeking her head through the open office door.

22

TAG

"Hello," I greet the jolly blonde behind the counter Sunday afternoon.

"Welcome to the ARL. How can I help you today?" She beams brightly.

"I'm actually looking to visit Emma," I state, scanning the area.

Two large glass windows flank the left and right side of the reception area. Through them I see kennels, but no humans. I notice the woman's name tag reads, "Hello, my name is Dawn."

"Oh my," she cackles. "Emma asked me to stay until two today." She glances at her wristwatch. "She's usually early, so I'd say... she will probably be here in thirty minutes or so." She smiles apologetically.

"That's okay," I inform her.

"You are welcome to wait if you want," Dawn offers. "You can roam around, or I could give you a tour."

Her hopeful face cons me into accepting her suggestion of a tour.

"Are you a cat or dog person?" she inquires.

I shrug. "I honestly don't know," I confess, having never owned a pet. "If I had to guess, I would say a dog person."

"I pegged you for a dog lover," she giggles. "Follow me." Dawn opens the large door on the right of the entranceway. "Currently we have over fifteen dogs waiting to find their forever homes."

I accepted an offer for a tour; I didn't say I was looking to rescue a dog. I barely step through the door before the scent of dogs and dog food assault my nose.

"On the left are our large dogs, and on the right are our smaller dogs," she states, resting her fingers on the metal cages, allowing the dogs to sniff and lick them. "All dogs are spayed or neutered, current on all shots…"

"I didn't expect to see so many," I think aloud.

Dawn pats my elbow. "We have many more currently fostered with volunteers. Those dogs are posted on our website."

"So, you have more dogs than you have room for?" I ask, my heart breaking a little.

"Unfortunately," she grimaces. "We are a no-kill shelter. Our volunteers and donors have big hearts. So, we attempt to foster animals until a permanent home can be found."

"Do you…"

She interrupts me, "I currently own two dogs and foster a cat." Pride is apparent on her face. "Before I gained custody of my infant niece, I fostered four to five at a time when needed. I have a large fenced-in backyard and my house is much too big for only me."

"That's amazing." I cannot imagine that to be an easy task. I have no frame of reference.

"How did Emma talk you into adopting?" Dawn asks, turning to face me at the end of the long hall with cages lining both walls floor to ceiling.

Suddenly, every dog barks, their noses pressed to their metal doors.

"That's our girl," Dawn announces, raising her voice over the loud barking. "She's a favorite of all our residents."

Unsure what she means, I furrow my brow. Dawn points to the door behind me. Spinning, I find Emma joins us in the dog paddock. While her hands are licked by nearby dogs, her wide blue eyes stare at me.

"What…?" She sputters.

"I will leave the two of you," Dawn states, slipping through a door behind her.

"What are you doing here?" Emma asks over the noise.

I take in the exuberant welcome her four-legged fans exude. A few dogs barked once or twice when Dawn and I walked in; their excitement for Emma is over the top. I am very interested in witnessing her interactions with these pets and uncovering the reason for their affection.

"I wanted to meet some of your furry friends," I explain with a shrug, suddenly worried I might have intruded by showing up unannounced.

"Really?" she smiles, her eyes sparkling in the fluorescent lighting.

I smile, "I had no idea there would be so many."

Her smile quirks on one side. "Unfortunately, there are some that we just can't help due to our limited space. We try to do the best we can."

"Do you have a favorite?" I ask, anxious to see her in action.

Emma pulls her lips between her teeth, attempting to hide her wide smile. She makes the come here motion with her index finger as she walks toward the center of the walkway. I move closer to her. When she places two hands on the upper kennel, a blonde dog laps at her fingertips, its paws pressed to the kennel bars.

"This is Bing," she informs. "He's been with us for 11 months now." She moves her face to the kennel bars, where Bing places a lick on the tip of her nose. "He likes to go for walks and plays fetch with me." As she talks, she opens the kennel door, lowering Bing to the concrete floor.

Bing ignores me, giving all his dog licks and paw presses to Emma.

"Bing, sit," she orders.

At first the dog continues to lick her while his short tail wags quickly.

"Bing, sit," she repeats, and this time he does sit in front of her.

Her attention moves to me now.

"Come say hi," she orders me from her crouched position in front of the dog.

I position myself beside her, squatting. Unsure of my next move, I look to Emma.

"Slowly extend your hand, fist closed, toward his nose," she states.

I follow her directions, allowing the dog to sniff my hand. Eventually, he darts his tongue out to lick my knuckles.

"He likes you," she giggles. "He wants you to pet him."

"Where?" Fear creeps in.

She will see my fear and instantly know I am not a dog person. My intention was to visit her at the shelter to see why she loves it so much, not for me to interact with the animals.

Emma doesn't answer. She places her hand on my wrist, guiding my hand to the top of Bing's ears. I slowly move my fingers to pet the soft, slightly curly hair. Bing leans into my touch, his eyes growing heavy. Moments pass then Emma urges my hand under his head. Now I rub his chin. Bing seems to like my touch.

"Ahh," Emma coos. "Usually, he's standoffish to men. He really likes you."

I think she tells me that to ease my fear. This dog must be friendly to everyone if he likes me.

"Do you pet dogs all day when you are here?" I ask, smiling so she knows I am teasing.

"Bing, let's go feed everyone," Emma says, standing and pointing towards the inside door Dawn disappeared through. "Let's go."

I follow Emma and Bing into a large back room. The dog begins running in circles around the large open space. I assume this is the indoor animal playground. I spot tires, children's plastic slides, and tennis balls scattered around the room.

"How can I help?" I offer.

Emma points me toward a fifty-gallon trash can, instructing me to remove the lid and fill a large bucket with kibble. As I carry the ten-gallon bucket of food, I wonder how she ever carries this weight. Emma opens each kennel, passing me the dish to fill, while she coos and pets the dog. Returning a full dish to each cage, we move on to the next one. Bing socializes with each of the lower kennels' tenants as we work. Once all fifteen dogs are fed, I lift Bing into his home and secure the latch.

"He's a Wowauzer," Emma states. "Part Schnauzer and part Welsh Terrier. His owner passed away, and her children didn't want to keep him." She turns her eyes from Bing to me. "He's almost been here a year."

I sense a year in a kennel is not good. Not wanting Emma to dwell on the sad situation of her little friend, I change the subject.

"Now what?" I ask.

"After they eat, I will walk each of them." Her eyes meet mine.

"Sixteen dogs is a lot of walks," I chuckle.

"Most of them I can walk three or four at a time," she explains. "It is the two new dogs that I am not sure how they will interact with the others."

This is not the easy volunteer job I expected it to be. Feeding the dogs and lifting them in and out of the cages is physical labor. There are many moving parts to every task she performs. The ARL is lucky to have someone young and fit; I doubt that Dawn could perform these same tasks.

"Did you bring a raincoat and umbrella," I inquire, still hearing the rain on the roof of the metal building.

Emma shakes her head. "I will let them loose in the indoor playground, and then pick up piles and piles of poo," she shares, wrinkling her nose. "Wanna help?"

I nod, causing her sweet blue eyes to widen. She thought she would scare me away with the dog poop. She was wrong. To spend time with her, I am willing to put up with the stench. She may make a dog lover out of me.

23

EMMA

"Promise you aren't mad at me?" Rachel asks for the umpteenth time since she returned.

"Rach, I'm not mad," I promise. "I wouldn't come over if I was. I'm happy you had a great weekend with a great guy."

"He is such a great guy," she gushes. "He totally gets me in every way. And the things he can do with his…"

"Oh! No!" I protest, covering my ears with my hands. "Don't tell me stuff like that about Justin. He is at my house all the time, and I don't need that in my head about him."

"I'm in loovvee," she claims with a swoon.

"Stop," I tease. "It's too soon. You need to take it slow and protect your heart."

"It's too late," she claims. "It only took twelve hours."

"This time," I grumble.

"Be nice," she chides. "You're supposed to be happy for me."

"Rach, I am happy for you. I just want you to be careful. I hate it when it doesn't work out, and you get hurt," I explain.

"And I love you for that." She hugs me. "So, what did you do while I was sexing it up with Justin?"

I roll my eyes at my friend. "I didn't do anything exciting," I answer.

"You're lying," she challenges.

"Why do you say that?" I worry.

"Something happened," she claims. "You… something just seems different. Maybe it's your smile."

"My smile?" I scoff.

"Did you hang out with Kate after the barbecue?" she inquires, and I shake my head.

"I watched movies and fell asleep in the theater room."

"By yourself?" she continues to interrogate.

I want to ignore this question. I don't want to divulge this truth.

"Not alone!" she squeals. "I knew it! Something did happen. I knew it!"

I feel the blush creep over my cheeks.

"Who did you hang out and watch movies with Saturday night?" she pries, growing more excited by the minute.

"We just watched movies," I tell her, making light of it all.

"Lies! You're lying. I can tell!" she points her index finger at my face.

"I watched movies with Tag Saturday night," I confess.

I've never witnessed Rachel's eyes so big.

"Oh. My. God." She drawls. "You have to tell me everything."

I shake my head. "We watched two movies. I fell asleep during the second one."

"Not buying it," she protests. "I can't believe you're trying to keep this from me."

"You promise not to make a big deal of it?" I ask, and she crosses her fingers.

"Tag offered to watch movies with me to thank me for helping him with his barbecue," I divulge.

"And…" she urges.

"And what?"

"Tell me what happened. There has to be more to it. You wouldn't need to hide the fact you only watched movies with Tag," she giggles, closing her bedroom door. "Now spill."

"I fell asleep during the second movie," I begin. "Instead of waking me up, Tag carried me to my bedroom. I woke up, and he kissed me. Like really kissed me." I search my friend's eyes for revulsion or disgust, but only find elation.

"Is he a good kisser? Was it slow and sweet or hot and promising hours of steamy sex?" Rachel talks a million miles a minute.

"Rach…" I interrupt. "Take a breath. It was a soft, sweet kiss. Lingering maybe. Then I said good night and he left. End of story."

"Not the end of story," Rachel proclaims. "It's easy to see that you liked the kiss. You're all glowy and smiley."

I am? I'm glowy? Do I want to be glowy?

"So, are you guys dating now?" she asks.

I feel my brow furrow. "I'm not sure what we are, really," I answer. "We're friends, I guess."

"Friends that kiss," she cheers. "Now we can double date."

"Rach… we are not dating. In fact, we both signed up for online dating and scheduled dates for Friday."

I see the air leak from her excitement bubble.

"Let me get this straight." She rises, arms folded across her chest. "You're becoming friends." She holds up one finger as she paces. "You kiss." She holds up a second finger as she walks back towards the bed from the window. "But you both decide to experiment with online dating." Back at the window, she stares outside. "Whose idea was the online dating?" Her eyes narrow on me from across the room. "It was your idea, wasn't it?" She jabs her index finger at me, closing the distance between us. "You're scared and you're running," she accuses. "You liked the kiss. You have new feelings for Tag, and you're trying to avoid them."

"He's my guardian, Rachel." I rise, now standing in front of her. "He's my step-uncle."

Rachel shakes her head fervently. "You're eighteen. You no longer need a guardian," she states. "And Tag was never your guardian. Bonnie was. So, get that out of your head. You're grasping for excuses." Rachel places her hands at my shoulders. "You're scared because of high school." Her eyes search mine. "You can trust Tag. Justin and I talked a lot about Tag this weekend. He's one of the good ones, Emma. You need to give him a chance."

I shake my head. "It doesn't matter. We're both going out with someone else on Friday night."

She huffs, frustrated. "So, show me this guy you're seeing on Friday. I need to make sure he is good enough for my girl."

24

TAG

I am ready for this horrible Friday night to end. My head swivels as I enter the restaurant. I find Emma and her date sitting in a booth against the far wall. I sidle up to the bar, attempting not to draw her attention. I am not at all happy with the selection of matches available to her. Although I chose who I found to be the best of them, I felt the need to check on her. It pleases me to see she sits opposite him in the booth with three-feet of table between them.

While he speaks animatedly, Emma swirls her green-striped paper straw in her water glass. She looks down at her straw and not her date. When a waitress approaches their table, he orders another drink; Emma shakes her head. She seems bored.

The bartender approaches, and I order a water, slipping him five dollars. I position my body to see Emma without constantly turning my head. I do not blatantly stare; I look to my water glass, the TV above the bar, then to her. I feel like a creep, watching her on her date.

When I could not take any more of my influencer date constantly on her cell phone, I made an excuse. Instead of driving home, I found a deep desire to peek in on Emma.

It's not that I want her date to be as miserable as mine; it's my distrust for the man I set her up with. He seemed to be the best of the worst, and I do not like her being alone with a twenty-five-year-old guy. I guess I have a problem with the age difference, even if she claims she does not.

On my next glance in her direction, I watch the man extend his arm across the table to touch her hand on her straw. She jerks her hand back as if he scalded her with his touch. I take that as a sign she is not into this guy. My mind scrambles for a way to make him leave without causing a scene. I call the bartender over and pull a crisp one-hundred-dollar bill from my money clip.

"I need your help to rescue my little sister," I lie. "See the girl over there in the booth."

I wait for him to nod.

"She is on a date from hell. Help me give her an excuse to leave. Can you tell her there is a phone call for her?"

He takes the landline phone off its cradle, before heading for Emma's booth. I watch as he interrupts the man still talking, and Emma hops up from her seat. Fear clouds her face as she hurries to the far end of the bar. I now regret making her worry.

The bartender leans close, and Emma's wide blue eyes dart to me. I watch her gaze morph to squinting eyes as the rest of her face pinches. I definitely crossed a line by checking on her.

She returns to her table, for her cell phone. She pulls cash from her pocket and places it on the table, waves to the guy, and walks out the front door.

Yep, she is pissed at me; I definitely overstepped the friendship, or what-ever we are, boundary.

I climb off my barstool, hurrying to follow after her. I find she is in the car, pulling from her parking spot. She does not look in my direction as she passes me at the edge of the lot. *She may be mad at me, but she is driving my Lexus. Maybe she will like it and finally allow me to purchase her an acceptable vehicle. Who am I kidding? She plans to rip me a new one when I get home.*

Emma

The house is dark except for a night light in the kitchen. The darkness reminds me that Bonnie and Barry drove to Iowa City to move Kate home from college this weekend.

I bee line to the freezer, grabbing a tub of chocolate peanut butter ice cream and a spoon before sitting on a kitchen stool. I waste no time lifting a heaping spoonful into my mouth.

What made me think online dating would be any better than the boys I dated in high school? For some reason, I thought older men would be more attentive, listen when I spoke, and cared about more than sex. I take a second bite hoping to erase the hour and a half of listening to him talk about his job, sports car, along with fishing and hunting trips. The sound of the door to the garage signals Tag's return. I don't look in that direction, instead I take another large bite of ice cream.

"I'm sorry," he says immediately, from behind me. "I wanted to pop in to make sure you were enjoying your date more than I did mine."

My eyes dart to him when he leans against the counter by the refrigerator in front of me. He does not smile or smirk; he seems sincere in his apology. I think I will let him squirm a bit before I confess, I am glad he rescued me.

"You didn't..." I begin to ask.

"No, I most certainly did not enjoy my date," Tag chuckles. "You should follow her on Instagram. She took several photos of our meal. Perhaps you could find new recipes."

"Stop it," I chide. "She is proud of her career."

"Career," he sneers. "Of all the influencers in Des Moines..."

"Tag, you are terrible. Businesses really do utilize influencers as a marketing strategy," I admonish.

"Let me finish," Tag directs. "Of all the influencers in the Des Moines area, I do not believe she will make a living at it. She does it for notoriety and not to promote the products. Trust me, she is on the hunt for 'a man of wealth'. Her words, not mine."

Tag places his hands under his chin and smiles sheepishly while batting his eyelashes, imitating his date.

I sputter, and the ice cream I swallowed sticks in my throat. Tag quickly pats his palm against my back until I stop coughing.

"I'm good, thank you."

Tag returns to his side of the island, pulling a spoon from the utensil drawer, then leans on the counter between us.

"May I?" he asks, spoon pointed towards my ice cream.

"Seems your date sucked as bad as mine," I say, sliding the tub to the center of the kitchen island between us. "Scale of one to ten, how bad?"

"Seven," Tag states between bites. "Yours?"

"Eight. Maybe a nine," I reply. "After boring me with his conversation for over an hour, he still hinted he thought I would award him with sex at the end of the date."

Tag

What. The. Fuck? Anger floods me; my veins feel full of molten lava. I knew I should not have gone through with setting her up. That is why I felt I needed to check on her after my date. *Guys suck.*

Bile climbs up my throat at the realization that I always expect sex at the end of a date. *I am such a hypocrite. Granted, I never had the pleasure of going out with someone as sweet and perfect as Emma.*

"TMI?" she asks, her spoon clinking against the marble countertop.

I shake my head, my anger and tumultuous thoughts too much for me to speak at the moment. I feel a strange need to keep Emma away from *all* men. Over the past two weeks, I feel a close relationship grew between us; the girl grew on me. With all I learned about her, I want to learn more—I need to learn more. *How did I not notice these things about her over the past three years?* I long to spend every free minute with her, make her smile, and make her laugh.

"Should we try again next week?" Emma asks, causing the bile to rise higher in my throat.

"How about we hang out together for a couple of weeks until the bitter taste of tonight's dates fade; then you ask me again," I offer.

She quirks a brow at me. I replay my words in my head. I meant we hang as friends; surely she knows I mean as friends. *I only want to be friends. Right?*

"I know I suggested it, but I rather not go on another one of *those* dates," Emma states, her cute little nose wrinkled like she smelled something rank.

"Thank god," I sigh loudly.

Together we laugh at our shared misery in the online dating pool.

"What should we do for the rest of the night?" Emma asks, tucking the tub of ice cream back into the freezer.

"Up for a movie?" I offer, hopeful.

"A comedy sounds perfect," she answers, and I cheer internally. "I'm gonna change. I'll meet you downstairs."

I watch Emma exit the kitchen, hanging back not to seem too eager. Bonnie's words of caution constantly play in my ears, "Let her lead and take it slow."

Once again, I allow Emma to pick our movie. She chose *The Hangover*, feeling I might need a break from her rom-coms. Unlike our previous movies, I have watched this one once before. I pop us popcorn while she grabs blankets and drinks.

"Popcorn makes every movie better," She professes between handfuls.

"Even horror movies?" I challenge, Emma shakes her head adamantly, and we share a laugh.

My cell phone vibrates on the seat beside me.

JUSTIN

chance of rain Sun

ME

slight chance

JUSTIN

I'll b there

ME

hang tom. night?

JUSTIN

prob b with Rachel

sorry dude

ME

(thumbs up emoji)

Emma glances at me, mouth full of popcorn.

"Justin," I explain.

She washes her food down with water before she asks, "Does he want to hang tonight?"

Even if he did, I would rather be here. I do not confess this to Emma.

"No, he's sharing the forecast for Sunday's golf," I share.

"The two of you doing anything tomorrow night? I might reach out to Rachel," she fishes.

I do not want her to get her hopes up. "Justin says he has plans tomorrow night with Rachel," I divulge.

Rolling her eyes, Emma releases a breath, causing her hair to flutter. It is adorable.

"I have a lunch meeting," I share.

"I need to record something." Her voice lacks enthusiasm. "This week is entrée week."

"If you wait til dinner, I could watch," I offer.

"Or... you could help," she counters. "My followers gushed over Justin and you from the cupcake footage of my birthday."

Warmth consumes me. She wants me to be a part of her career, like I enjoy her helping me with mine. While I do not particularly care for standing in front of the camera, I do enjoy cooking with her, and I am beginning to realize I will endure almost anything to be near her.

"What's for dinner?" I ask, agreeing to posing as her partner for the next filming.

25

TAG

The kitchen is truly Emma's domain. While I struggle dicing the tomatoes as instructed on the cutting board, she rattles off seasonings, and it sounds like a foreign language to me. She tells me the names of each pan and utensil, and my mind scrambles to remember some of them. I detest feeling inept.

"When you are done," Emma instructs, her back to me. "Place them in the pot."

"Do you always make homemade marinara?" I ask, cutting two more times before scraping the cutting board into the pot she pointed to.

"Yep," she answers, popping her 'p'. "Nothing beats fresh tomatoes."

I pay more attention around my house these days. As I contemplate Emma's words, I open the dishwasher door and place my knife with the board in as I witnessed Bonnie and Emma often do. I glance toward Emma for approval. When she nods, my chest swells a bit. *I am learning.*

While I tend to the chicken on the stove top, Emma pours part of her homemade marinara in the bottom of a baking dish.

"What is my next task?" I ask, approaching her from behind.

I watch in silence as she dips the chicken into flour, an egg mixture, then breadcrumbs.

"Now, you can sauté the chicken, four minutes on each side, until golden brown," she says, handing the breaded chicken to me. "The skillet is hot."

I marvel that I no longer notice the movement of the cameras as we complete our tasks.

"I think this is done," I state, hoping for her confirmation.

"Yep. Now lay the chicken breasts on top of the sauce."

I lay each piece of chicken in the baking dish, then lean against the counter as Emma paints the rest of the marinara on top. Next, she covers each with freshly grated mozzarella cheese and sprinkles seasonings with her fingers over the entire dish.

"How long will it bake?" I ask, watching her slide the dish into the hot oven.

"Fifteen minutes," she smiles, our task complete for the moment. "Let's clean the kitchen and get our plates ready."

"We make a good team," she claims, dabbing the corner of her mouth with her napkin.

"I think you mean to say you are an excellent chef, and I cut tomatoes okay," I tease.

"You sautéed the chicken, too," she reminds me.

I nod as I chew my next bite.

"I hope I didn't screw up your video," I say, then wish I kept that thought to myself.

Emma takes a sip of water before she responds. "Don't be silly. I edit the footage. I'll be sure you look dashing for my fans."

Taking a page from her playbook, I roll my eyes.

"You have fangirls asking me for your contact info," she laughs.

I choose to play it cool, making light of her comment and my feelings. "Maybe one of them will be better than my online date was."

Emma chortles. Her laughter bounces off the walls of the pool house. When she snorts, I join in.

Emma's eyes lock on mine; their warm depths draw me in.

"Tag," she murmurs.

Oh no! Here it comes; she plans to rebuff me.

"Shh," I prompt, placing my finger to her lips. "I know what you want to say."

Her forehead scrunches.

"You want to talk about our kiss. You worry what others might think of us being step relatives. I do not foresee that as an issue. Barry, Bonnie, Kate, Justin, Rachel, and the old cronies at the firm are the only ones that know paperwork listed me as your step-uncle. Our family and friends want us to be happy. They will not let a legal document keep us from happiness. As for the men at the firm—who cares? They do not care for us personally, only financially. What matters is you and me. If we are happy…"

"But Bonnie will…" she starts to interrupt.

"I told Bonnie about our kiss the next morning," I confess.

Her eyes bug out.

"She is a mother to me," I remind Emma. "She advised me to take it slow and follow your lead." I watch her face as my words sink in.

"So, what do you want to do?" Emma asks.

I place my hand on hers. "I need to know how you feel and what you want," I answer and hold my breath.

Several silent seconds pass.

"I like the Tag I've spent time with the past two weeks," she states in a low voice.

"I like the Tag that you encouraged me to become," I admit.

Silence fills the kitchen again.

"Did you like…" I begin to ask.

"I liked…" Emma says at the same time.

We laugh.

"You first," I encourage, hopeful.

A sweet smile forms, and her eyes twinkle in the overhead lighting. "It was okay," she attempts to state, but loses her battle with laughter.

"Just okay, huh?" I chuckle.

It guts me Justin kissed her.

"I wanna say 'I've had better', but I am not that good of a liar," Emma grins.

"So… I am the best kisser?" I pry.

"Well, I have a very small pool to compare it to," she murmurs, embarrassed.

I like the thought that she has not kissed many guys.

"Are we dating?" she blurts. "I mean, I know you don't date. So, where does this leave us?"

I wet my lips between my teeth before I speak. "I have not found the right woman to date, but I am open to it when it feels right." I want to add I am open to dating her but worry my boldness might scare her away. "I am eager to spend time with you. I will not be going out with another woman as long as you are interested in me. I have thought of no one but you for over a week. It is new for me, and I like it."

Emma bites the corner of her lip and fiddles with her thumb nail while I speak. When I finish, she looks up at me through her lashes. Slowly her mouth morphs into a smile. She places her hand beside mine allowing our pinky fingers to touch.

"Let's load the dishwasher," she prompts, catching me off guard.

I replay her words, sure I misheard her.

"What?" she laughs. "This isn't our first date."

I shake my head at her quirkiness.

"I planned to help you with the dishes, and I do count this as a date," I inform her. I round the island, finding her eyes wide as saucers. I make a mental note that Emma would like a date where she does not cook sometime soon.

"Do you want to edit your video tonight?" I ask, wiping down the counters as she starts the dishwasher.

"Nah, I'm not in the mood," she states. "Movie sounds good. I'm ready to relax."

Emma

Changed, I make my way toward the stairs. Noticing a light still on in Tag's room, I walk in that direction.

"I think I'm in the mood for a drink tonight," I announce, standing in the doorway to his bedroom.

Tag's hands freeze on the hem of his t-shirt he recently pulled over his head. My eyes remain distracted at his waist.

"I have beer in my mini fridge," he offers. "We could hang out in here tonight." I follow his hand as he points to the sitting area near his fireplace. "I'm not insinuating we will..." Tag looks behind him toward his giant bed.

"We could watch TV in here," I agree. "And I wouldn't turn down a beer."

I take a seat on the small sofa in the seating area, while Tag fetches two beers before joining me.

"You know the drill; find us a movie," he prompts.

I pull up *The Hangover Part II*, deciding to continue through that trilogy.

"You know I am contributing to the delinquency of a minor," he teases, pointing his beer bottle towards mine.

"Whatever. I have no doubt you drank prior to your twenty-first birthday," I return.

"Touché," he quips.

I press play, starting our movie, and we watch in silence as the sun sets outside Tag's bedroom window.

26

TAG

The air thickens the closer our movie draws to its end. From the moment in the middle of the movie when I encouraged her to scoot closer to me, I struggled focusing on the show. My arm around her, at first my hand played with her hair. Now, my fingers fiddle with the hem of her top. Her head rests against my shoulder, and her sweet scent invades my nostrils.

The credits fill the screen. Emma leans forward, takes the remote in hand, and proceeds to turn the television off. Still beside me, she turns towards me. Her eyes hone in on my mouth and urges me to wet my lips. They follow the movement of my tongue.

"Emma," my gruff voice signals my waning restraint.

"Hmm?" she returns focusing on my mouth.

"I want to kiss you," I growl.

"Okay." Her lust-filled eyes meet mine.

I waste no time melding my mouth to hers. Unlike our sweet first kiss, this time my kiss conveys the lust she stirs within me. I nip her lower lip playfully; her gasp spurs me on. I dart my tongue out to swipe the crease between her lips. She parts for me, inviting me inside. Slowly my tongue caresses hers. My hands on her cheeks, I tip her head, deepening our kiss. Her fingers fisting in the bottom of my shirt signal me to continue. My thumbs caress the soft skin of her jawline as I continue to explore her mouth. At her fingertips trailing their way past my waistband, my abdominal muscles clinch.

Due to Bonnie's warning to proceed slowly, I only hoped to kiss Emma this evening. Emma's bold move to my groin shocks me. My erection grows exponentially with her hand moving over it, and I find it harder and harder to restrain my need for her.

Our kiss heats with each stroke Emma rewards me. I fight the urge to remove my shorts and thrust against her palm. I try to focus on her mouth, as well as puppies and finance numbers to quell my raging hard on. But Emma's slender fingers gripping my cock through my shorts causes my balls to tighten and sparks to zing down my spine. I'm gonna lose my load too soon. *How do I not hurt her feelings, removing her hand?*

"Emm," I moan, placing my hand on top of hers. "Honey your touch is… too much for me."

Grabbing her wrist, I guide her hand to my mouth, kissing each of her fingers, her palm, then the back of her hand.

"I don't want to cum in my shorts," I explain, my voice husky. "I have too many things I want to do with you."

Her tongue licks her lower lip before she bites it. Reading all her signals, I scoop her up, carrying her to my bed. On my mattress, Emma removes her t-shirt. Wasting no time, I kiss my way between the swell of her breasts, over her navel, down further still, detouring to her right thigh at the last moment. I can feel her frustration of my being so close to where she wants me. I slide my hands from her knees up her thighs, pausing mere inches from her center.

"Tag, please," she begs, shifting her hips towards me.

Tucking my fingers in her waistband, I slide her sleep shorts and panties toward her feet. Urging her to open for me. I smile wickedly at her before dipping my face between her thighs.

Opening her up with my thumbs, I swipe my tongue slowly, pausing to swirl on her clit, then prepare to repeat the motion. Emma's low drawn-out moan spurs me to continue. I keep my eyes cast upwards, while I focus my attention on the titillating task in front of me. I nip, I lick, and I suck her inner thighs, her lips, and her hard nub.

"Taaggg," she rasps. "Don't stop."

I'm happy to oblige. When she begins to wriggle and writhe beneath me, I lay one forearm across her abdomen to hold her still.

"Mm-hmm."

I continue my oral assault on the most sensitive parts of her.

"Mmm-hmm," she groans.

Sensing she's close, I focus my mouth on her clit, pressing it with the tip of my tongue, then swirling it, while sliding two fingers inside her. Instantly, her inner walls constrict, signaling an orgasm. Wiggling my fingers, I gently suck her clit, pushing her over the edge.

"Oh god! Oh god!" She chants, her inner walls spasming around my fingers.

I continue caressing her inner walls, drawing out her orgasm for long moments before I nip her inner thigh, withdrawing my fingers, before crawling up her body. Emma's chest heaves, her lips are parted, and eyes closed. When I fall to the mattress beside her, she opens her eyes, turning her head toward me. I trail my fingertips up and down her ribcage, admiring Emma's sated beauty.

She places her hand upon my cheek. "Amazing," she murmurs.

I chuckle at her lazy speech.

Emma

So, this is what I've been missing. Oh. My. God. I mean, this man has a magical mouth. And why haven't I ever allowed a guy to go downtown before? Wow!

I freeze; sound penetrates our bubble.

"What's that?" I bolt upright, fear washing over me.

"Storm sirens," Tag states, placing his hand on my shoulder. "It's just the storm sirens."

"I...I..." Scrambling from the bed, I open the top dresser drawer, snagging a pair of Tag's boxer briefs, and then another grabbing a t-shirt. I'm slipping them on as I look to him, still on the bed. "I... storms."

Tag seems to scoot off his bed in super, slow motion.

"Forecast predicted a thunderstorm tonight. I'm sure the sirens are for high winds or hail."

How can he be so calm?

"The sirens..." I gulp in a breath. "We need... the basement. Now!"

Brow furrowed, Tag stares at me a moment. "Let's head to the media room. I'll turn on the weather."

He places his hand on the small of my back, guiding me from his room.

Tag

I feel like an ass. Emma has lived under my roof for three years, and I didn't know she had an irrational fear of storms. I feel ill-equipped to help with her current anxiety, panic, and fear. On all the phone calls I made to Mona, she neglected to share Emma's phobia with me.

With the local station on the big screen, we learn the sirens warn of winds in excess of 50 mph associated with this storm. I hold her tight to my side, her head pressed to my chest as I listen to the weather and local radar reports.

"We now have reports of a tornado touching down near Van

Meter in Dallas County. We're tracking movement of this system heading due east. Residents in Dallas and Polk County should immediately take cover…"

I'm unable to hear the meteorologist over Emma's wails.

"We're going to die! We're going to die!" She screams.

"Shh, Emma. Honey, we're safe in the basement with no windows," I attempt to calm her.

It's futile as she can't hear me over her own screams. I take her head from my chest in my two hands.

"Emma, we're safe…"

I do not finish my statement because the power goes out.

No! I lose my battle; I can't calm her as the storm ramps up. I decide the best thing I can do is hold her and keep her warm. I move her onto my lap, lay a blanket over her shoulders, and wrap my arms tightly around her. She buries her face in the crook of my neck; I can feel her hot tears. Her lips moving, listening closely I can tell she's chanting something but can't make it out.

"The generator should kick on any minute," I murmur into her hair, my hand rubbing her back. As if on cue, the lights flicker on. I extend my arm, reaching for the remote to turn the radar reports back on.

"Don't leave me!" She squeals, panicking with my movement.

"Just getting the re…"

A loud, constant, rolling rumble surrounds the house. I swear I can feel the house shaking.

Pop!

The power goes out again, as the rolling rumble continues. I assume something hit the generator.

"I should go out and fix the generator," I tell Emma.

"No!" She shouts, attempting to bury her head deep through the wall of my chest. "Don't leave me."

I snag another throw blanket and a nearby pillow, laying us down and settling myself beside her. Emma's in the fetal position, head to my chest. I pull her tight to me, wrapping my arms around her.

Fifteen minutes later the rumbling ceases; I'm still holding a shivering Emma. She jumps with each crack of lightning and boom of thunder. Approximately thirty minutes later, the sounds of the storms wane. Shortly after that, Emma falls asleep in my arms. The power is still off, I decide to settle in for sleep.

27

TAG

"Why is she deathly afraid of storms?" I ask between bites.

Bonnie shakes off my question.

"Bonnie," I urge. "How can I help her if I don't know what triggers it?"

Still nothing from Bonnie as she busies herself putting ingredients back into the cabinets.

"Did her dad die during a storm?" I attempt to get some sort of response.

Bonnie freezes with eggs in her hands, facing me on the opposite side of the island. I find conflict in her eyes. I can see she wants to tell me, but she doesn't want to break Emma's confidence.

"Has she seen a therapist? You mentioned medication. Give me something," I plead.

Bonnie quickly places items in the refrigerator before leaning her forearms on the counter between us. She releases a heavy sigh.

In a low voice she shares, "Two years ago, in the spring, the art department worked after school on a mural to use at prom. For a couple of weeks, she spent an hour to two with other students drawing then painting the large design. It's all that she and Rachel talked about; they were very excited to be chosen. At the time the two constantly sketched and painted, posting their finished projects online for sale." Under her breath she shares, "If you ask me, Emma is much more talented than Rachel. She won a few local art awards and even had people commission her to paint works for them."

I had no idea. I search my brain but cannot recollect a single art project I knew of. I try to remember the art Frank displayed around the house and in his office. *Nothing.* Even now, I don't see her art displayed even in her bedroom.

"The Tuesday before prom, Rachel had an orthodontist appointment after school. Emma worked on the project and planned for Barry to pick her up at five." Bonnie pauses, taking two deep breaths. "A thunderstorm moved through the area. It was one of those fast-approaching, super storms."

I spot tears forming in Bonnie's eyes. A pit forms in my stomach. It feels like a red-hot fire poker pierces my gut. Instinct tells me this has little to do with the weather.

"The art teacher worked in the classroom, while his students worked in the commons where there was more room to spread out," Bonnie's voice shakes more and more as she retells this story. "When the storm sirens sounded, Emma and the two boys took shelter in a nearby janitor's office."

Bile rises from the fire in my abdomen. I struggle to breathe; the air in the room grows heavy. I fear I know. The urge to growl consumes me.

"The three of them could not hear the storm sirens in the office, but they tracked everything on the radar app on Emma's phone. When her phone battery died, Emma felt the worst of the storm had passed and made to leave the office."

Bonnie no longer looks me in the eye. Now her head lowers and she picks at her cuticles. I watch her fingers fiddle nervously as she attempts to continue.

"From what she shared with me, one of the boys stood in front of the door blocking her escape." Bonnie returns to her previous task, clearing her workspace and wiping down every countertop.

"Bonnie," I force out with a gravelly voice.

Back toward me, she freezes.

"I need to know," I state.

"You won't like it," she informs, still not turning toward me.

"I knew I wouldn't like it when I asked about the storms," I tell her. "My mind is running wild with every horrible scenario. I need to know," I say firmly.

"They assaulted her," she blurts, head low, hands gripping the edge of the counter.

My lips snarl as my fingers curl into fists.

"Emma couldn't share all the details. I encouraged her to open up to her therapist and she claims she did." Bonnie spins to face me, pressing her fingers tight to the counter's edge at her sides. "One boy held her arms behind her back while the other... touched her. She fought back. She thinks she kicked them both in the crotch, causing them to bend over, and that is when she was able to open the door and run away.

I can't look away; my eyes implore Bonnie to continue with this horrifying story.

"It was late, so the school was almost empty. Her cell phone battery was dead. She ran to the office, but the door was locked. She ran to the art room, but she didn't find the teacher there. She yelled for help as she ran through the halls. The teacher came from the men's restroom where he took shelter from the storm. He called 9-1-1."

"Barry and I waited in the parking lot as the rain poured down. At first we thought nothing of the police car parked near the door, but the longer we waited, the more it seemed wrong. Emma is prompt; if she says five, she walks out the door at five. We hurried through the rain. Inside the school, we found the officers and the art teacher standing in front of Emma as she sat at a lunch table."

"Barry asked the three men why they were questioning her without a guardian present." Bonnie wipes tears from her plump cheeks.

I rise from my stool, wrapping her in my arms. Immediately, she buries her face in my chest.

Her voice muffled, she continues, "Emma filed a police report.

The officers searched the school and parking lot, but the two boys were already gone."

"Did they..." I clear my throat. "Did they ra..."

"No," Bonnie shakes her head against my chest as she explains through her sobs. "They touched and restrained... She fought back... got away before..." her voice trails off.

I breathe a slight sigh of relief. I detest everything she experienced. *It could have been much worse. She fought. Thank God she fought; thank God she escaped.*

I am such an ass; I am a selfish prick. I lived my life at college never caring about Emma's life here in Des Moines. I felt she was a nuisance and not important. While I played football, partied, and loved my life in Iowa City, she was assaulted by two boys with no parents to help her.

"I am sorry," I murmur. "I am sorry I wasn't here. I am sorry I didn't help."

Bonnie pulls back, looking up to me through her wet lashes.

"There was nothing to do. Once we helped her file the police report, the only thing we could do was make her therapy appointments, check in on her often, and attempt to carry on as we had before," Bonnie shares. "It's a helpless feeling, trying to help but having nothing you can do."

"At least you were here for her," I mutter. "You know how to help her prepare for storms, you know everything, and I know next to nothing."

"That is changing," Bonnie murmurs. "The two of you are talking and hanging out." She pats my shoulder. "You both need that."

I roll my eyes at her motherly tone emerging.

She swats my chest as she pulls away.

"You better get to work, and I need to get things done in here before Barry and Emma walk in," she shoos me off, ready to leave this dark topic of conversation.

I place a peck on her cheek before I leave the kitchen. My mind swirls as anger pulses through me. So many questions, and I want answers. *Where are the two little shits right now? What punishment did they receive? Years later, Emma still suffers; I long to make them suffer— suffer now and for years to come.* Evil ideas play out in my head. *Work will have to wait; I need to swim laps to clear my thoughts.*

28

EMMA

I draw in a long breath, my entire body aches. I stretch my legs and arms, opening my eyes. I'm alone in the pitch-black room. I fight the aches of every muscle, sitting up. I'm in the basement media room. *The power must still be out.*

I scoot off the recliner, curling my toes in the carpet below. My knees crackle when I stand. *What a night.* Ascending the stairs to the ground level, each step brings with it more light. I'm thankful for the large windows throughout the house, providing light in place of the electricity. I follow the faint sounds of chatter to the kitchen.

"You're up," Bonnie greets, a worried smile upon her face. "Rough night, honey." She wraps me in a bear hug. "I'm sorry I wasn't here for you."

"What time is it?" I garble against her shoulder.

"Nearly eleven," she shares, holding me at arm's length. "Did Tag take good care of you?"

I'm embarrassed. *I'm a grown-ass woman. I shouldn't need to be taken care of during storms.* Last night was worse than usual; I made several mistakes.

"Emma?" Bonnie's worried tone draws me back.

"He did everything he could do to help me," I inform her. It's the truth. I was ill-prepared for the storm last night, and that included my not sharing my astraphobia and brontophobia with him.

"Why's the power still out?" I ask as I take the iced coffee she offers me.

"A tree fell on the generator. Another tree fell on the pool fence and another on the roof of the garage," she shares. "Tag and Barry assessed the damage and have called to get them fixed."

"Barry will have a busy day, I'm sorry you had to come home early." I rise from my stool to peek out the window toward the garage.

"We were packed and ready," Bonnie states. "Honestly, I was ready to come home yesterday." She holds her index finger to her lips, asking me to keep that secret.

"I think I'll relax for a bit before I head to work at three," I inform her, coffee in hand, heading toward my bedroom.

I look toward Tag's office on my way by the foyer, finding his door closed. *I wonder if he's working in there today or if he drove to the firm?* I shrug to myself; it doesn't matter. He has work to do, and I have a shift tonight. *After my freak out during the storms, I'm sure he's done with me.*

Closing my bedroom door, I just now realize Bonnie saw me in Tag's t-shirt and boxers. I blush at the assumptions she surely made. *Oh well, we've talked about Tag and I growing closer.*

I climb under my covers, my current book in hand. I have two hours until I need to shower and dress for my doctor's appointment then work. I plan to read and perhaps squeeze in a quick nap. I set an alarm on my cell phone and open my novel.

Two chapters in, someone knocks on my door.

"Come in," I call.

"Lunch time," Bonnie announces, tray in hand.

I open my mouth to protest, but she has none of it.

"I know you only woke up an hour ago, but it is after noon," she argues. "I won't have you go to work on an empty stomach."

I find a burger and fries on the tray with a bottle of water. "How'd you cook with no power?"

"Barry started the grill for me," she smiles, proud of her intuitiveness.

"Awesome," I praise, burger in hand, suddenly aware I am starving.

"Kate asked me to tell you she plans to hang by the pool this weekend, if you want to join her to catch up," Bonnie states, doorknob in hand.

"Sounds good," I answer before she exits.

I look forward to spending a week with Kate catching up before she heads to her semester abroad. Moving in after my mother passed away, finding Bonnie and Barry had a daughter, living on the premises, seemed a godsend. Bonnie filled the role of mother in my life, and Kate my older, adopted sister.

Tag

I dropped the ball. I'm a freaking idiot. I emerge from my office at five, on a mission to find Emma. Peering out the French doors, she's not at the pool; I walk upstairs to her wing, but she is not in her bedroom. *Hmm. Bonnie. She'll know where to find her.*

Bonnie scurries around the kitchen preparing a meal and … I'm not sure what all the extra ingredients and devices on the island are for.

"Hey," she greets.

"What's all this?" I ask, trying to play it cool.

Bonnie wipes white powder on her floral apron, smiling at me when she turns. "Salmon Spud salad," she brags. "I'm trying something new. It has green beans, asparagus, spinach, potatoes, and tomatoes. It's a full meal in one dish."

"Nice," I reply, not even caring about food right now.

"This mess will be macaroons," she adds, hand sweeping above the pastry ingredients on the island.

"Going all out," I state.

"Kate's rarely home, so I'm trying to make it special," she beams.

"Spending time with Barry and you is all she needs to make it special," I channel Bonnie's usual words of wisdom for me. I fiddle with tongs on the counter in front of me.

"She's at work tonight," Bonnie grins. When my eyes dart to hers, she continues, "It's what you really came in here to find out."

Her knowing smile makes me chuckle.

"Dinner at seven," Bonnie reminds me of our usual dinner time.

"I'll be there," I tell her, hiding my disappointment that Emma will not be with us this evening.

The night drags on. At ten-thirty I make my way to the pool, hoping laps will distract me for an hour. I need to clear my head of Emma moaning in my bed, of trauma that brought on her fear of storms, and of holding her all night in my arms.

Thankfully last night's storm didn't damage the pool, I toss a towel on the nearest lounge chair, tie the string at the waist of my trunks, then dive into the clear water. The water temperature cools me instantly on this hot, June night.

Lap after lap, I beg my mind to clear and my heart to stop hurting. I'm not sure how I messed up last night, but I had to do something that caused her to avoid me all day today. *Maybe I said the wrong thing when she was afraid last night. Or was it the oral? She didn't fake her orgasm. No. Did she fake her orgasm? Laps. Laps. Focus on laps, not on Emma.*

Emma

. . .

Longest day ever. Finally home, I grab a water from the refrigerator before I search for Tag; I owe him an apology. His office door is open, so he's not in there. *Wait.* The pool lights are on. I walk to the French doors overlooking the patio and pool. I lean my forehead against the cool glass windowpane, my eyes following Tag as he swims over and back, over and back.

I'm bone tired. My anxiety from last night's storm took everything out of me. I place my palm flat to the window. *Goodnight Tag, Let's talk tomorrow.* I pull my forehead from the glass, trudging my way to my room.

I'm too tired to shower; I usually wash away the grease and food smells. I'm too tired to wash my face and brush my teeth. I'm too tired to find pajamas; I strip naked and slide into bed. *I desperately want to talk to Tag. Check that, I need him to hold me.* I close my eyes, imagining him holding me as he did last night. Immediately I fall asleep.

Tag

Toweled dry, I glance at my cell phone. It's nearly midnight. *I wonder if Emma's home yet?* I lock the French doors, making my way to the kitchen for water. I hate this house when it's quiet; it's much too big for Emma and me. When I invited Bonnie and her family to move in, I hoped that would liven the place up. Unfortunately, this house, with its thirty rooms, is still too big for the five of us.

I climb the stairs, turn to the right, and head down Emma's hallway. It hits me: I have no idea what time the restaurant Emma works at closes. I slow my steps in case she made it home and fell asleep as I swam. I approach her closed bedroom door, press my ear against it, listening and hoping noise alerts me she's awake inside.

Hearing nothing, my hand turns her doorknob. I peek my head in. I see her silhouette lying under a sheet, on her bed.

It's been a long day without interacting with her. Something inside me won't allow me to close the door. I step inside, tiptoeing to the side of her bed. I must see her; I can't end my day without her. Coming around the far side of her bed, the faint moonlight filters through her windows, casting shadows upon her face and…

I freeze. Her sheet rests over the curve of her hip, her bare torso on display. Every part of me longs to slide into bed with her, to trail my fingers over her smooth skin, and feel the weight of her breasts in my hands. The taste she awarded me before the storm last night was not enough. I'm already addicted; I'll never get enough of her. I gently tug the sheet up to her shoulder before reluctantly exiting her room.

In my bathroom, I step out of my still-damp swim trunks and shower before slipping under my covers. I fluff my pillow, lying on my back as I do every night to sleep. Long moments pass. I turn to one side then the other, I turn on the ceiling fan, and even attempt to lay on my stomach, but sleep refuses to visit me.

Emma consumes my thoughts. Her bare breasts burn in my brain. I contemplate fisting my cock but fight the urge. I can't make it a daily habit. Instead, I pull a notepad and pen from my bedside table, turn on my lamp, and prop myself on a second pillow. I jot a quick note to Emma, unable to let midnight come without me attempting to communicate with her.

Note complete, I quietly slip into her bedroom once again, leaning it against her cell phone on her nightstand. I hope it's the first thing she sees tomorrow morning. I retreat through the silent hallways back to my bedroom. Having shared my message with Emma, now Mr. Sandman escorts me to a dreamland.

29

EMMA

I wake to bright sunlight streaming through my two large windows. I forgot to close the drapes last night. I sit up against my headboard, the sheet falling from my shoulders to my waist. The cool air alerts me to my naked chest. I shake my head, remembering I was too tired to shower and change last night.

Reaching for my cell phone, my hand freezing midair when I notice the paper tented upon it. My fingertips trace my name scribed on it. It's not Bonnie or Kate's handwriting; it's unfamiliar. I bite my lips in anticipation, slowly unfolding it.

Emma,

I couldn't let the day pass without seeing you. I hope you'll excuse my sneaking into your bedroom while you slept. Thoughts of you kept me going all day, but pale in comparison to the reality of my eyes upon you. Please forgive my middle-school antics. Since I couldn't speak to you, I had to write you a note. I hope to see you tomorrow/today; I should be free after 3.

Yours,
Tag

I feel silly for my worries yesterday, that he learned I wasn't worth his trouble when I freaked out during the storm. I shake my head.

He wrote me a note. I grin like a middle-school girl. With my bedroom door closed, he could have simply texted me, but he took the time to write me a note and sneak into my bedroom. My wide smile spreads warmth into every cell of my body.

Climbing from bed, I shower and dress for breakfast, a skip in my step.

"Good morning," I greet Bonnie as I slide onto a stool at the kitchen island.

Smiling, she slides a bowl of yogurt and fresh cut fruit in front of me. I roll my eyes, instead of arguing with her. She's only following Tag's instructions that I eat breakfast before I consume my iced coffee.

"Will Tag be down soon?" She asks me.

My brow furrows as I shrug.

"Hmm," she turns back to the bacon in her skillet. "I haven't heard or seen him yet this morning. His bedroom door is closed, but I assumed he was sleeping late with you."

Late? I wouldn't call 7:30 late, but Tag's an early riser. I can't think of any time that he wasn't up working or at least eating breakfast when I got up. I remember him swimming laps at eleven, but swimming laps into the wee hours of the morning is not unusual for him. I quirk my lips to the side as I ponder this.

Wait! Did she really say, "sleeping late with you"? Does she think the two of us are sleeping together now? I continue to quietly freak out at her nonchalance at Tag and me having sex.

"I'll give him thirty more minutes," she states. "Then I'll knock on his door to make sure he isn't ill."

At that exact moment we hear a door loudly close. I look to Bonnie, and she looks to me. We both pull our lips between our teeth, attempting to hide our grins. Clearly, he's angry he slept in and plans to skip breakfast, heading straight to his office.

"Fix his breakfast," I tell Bonnie. "I'll risk my life delivering it to his desk."

We laugh.

"Better you than me," she chuckles, causing me to worry.

I wonder if he struggled falling asleep after he dropped the note off in my room. A part of me likes the idea that he loses sleep over thoughts of me. Perhaps I consume his thoughts as he consumes mine.

With his breakfast in hand, I make my way to Tag's office door. I knock lightly three times.

"Come in," Tag calls.

I peek my head in first, making sure he's okay with my presence. Phone in his right hand at his ear, he waves me in with his left. He continues his phone call, eyes glued to me. He mouths "thank you".

I place the plate on his desk, nervously wave, and exit as quickly as I entered. On the other side of his closed office door, I exhale a heavy breath. He seemed happy to see me. Maybe everything is okay between the two of us.

30

EMMA

The morning passes quickly, and soon Kate and I enjoy the hot summer sun in the pool after lunch. Sitting at the pool's edge, our feet and calves dangling in the water, we allow the warm sun to kiss our exposed skin.

"So..." Kate draws out, her shoulder nudging mine. "You and Tag... how long has this been a thing?"

I shake my head. "We've just been talking and hanging out," I share.

"I'm not buying it," she states. "The way the two of you light up in each other's presence hints to more. Much more."

I shrug. "There's nothing to tell."

Internally, I struggle with my words. I'm still not sure. *Is there something more? Are we a thing? A couple?*

"Have you kissed?" Kate pries, eyebrows waggling. "You have!" She points to my face. "You're blushing."

I close my eyes for a moment, not sure whether I should share. *I mean, is there anything to share?*

"He's a good kisser, isn't he?" she urges.

I feel my eyes widen as I worry my lip. *Why do both Rachel and Kate know Tag excels at kissing?*

"I knew it!" She squeals. "Oh. My. God. I fantasized about Tag so many times in high school and even away at college. You lucky girl!"

"Shh," I blush. "Not so loud."

"Details. Now." Kate demands. "From the beginning. I want to hear it all."

I close my eyes, exhaling in preparation. "I had a meeting with the finance guys for my eighteenth birthday," I begin, rolling my eyes. "Tag drove me to a dinner one of the partners planned." I shake my head. "I think they felt they owed it to Grandfather to make it a dinner instead of a meeting in the boardroom." I shrug.

"It blindsided me," I admit. "I mean, I knew Grandfather had set up a trust fund for me, but I had no idea how large it was. Add to that the money my mom set up… I excused myself from the meeting, throwing up in the bathroom."

Kate's hand rubs up and down my bare back. "My parents worked for your grandfather, so I knew he had money. It wasn't until Tag invited us to move into the apartment above the garage after your mother passed that I started to fathom the amount of money your family had." She bends her head, aligning her eyes with mine. "Your mom and you never put off the 'I have money' vibe. I love that about you. It made it easier to think of you as my sister." She wraps an arm around my shoulder, hugging me to her side.

"Even I had no idea the amount," I admit, shaking my head. "Weeks later, it still feels surreal."

"What happened after that meeting?" She asks, seeking the details of Tag kissing me.

"Tag apologized," I share. "I think it hit him that night how much I lost, how young I was back when Mom passed, and how lost I am."

"He opened up. From that night on, we've talked more than we did in the prior three years combined." I rise from the pool's edge, applying more sunscreen and offering it to Kate.

"The more we talked, the more time we spent together," I tell her. "It caught me off guard when he kissed me. So many emotions and worries flooded my brain that I almost missed out on all the awesomeness of the kiss." I blush.

"What worries?" Kate inquires.

"He's my step-uncle," I state the obvious.

"No, he's not," she rebuts. "He's a guy whose mother married your grandfather. You weren't raised as a family. Your step-uncle didn't attend your birthday or Christmas parties. Essentially, you were strangers under the same roof until weeks ago." She bends to eye level, forcing me to acknowledge her words.

"Not everyone will see it that way," I argue.

"Not everyone knows your mom signed a document asking him to serve as a guardian for three years," she counters. "It only matters what you two think and feel. It's a brutal world. You need to cling to happiness when you find it."

My brow furrows. *"A brutal world." What is she talking about? Did something happen to her?*

"You're eighteen now," she continues. "Grown-ass women take control. They go for what they want; if they want happiness, they do everything in their power to stay happy. You like hanging with Tag. He makes you happy. You have chemistry. Don't get hung up on what you think others might think. If you want him, go for it." She watches me. When I don't speak, she pushes my shoulder. "What?" She pries.

"We set up dates for one another online with a person we thought would be a perfect match." I chuckle at the memory. "Needless to say, our blind dates sucked. Tag actually rescued me from mine. That's when we decided to see what might..."

"And..." she prods. "You're in love, getting married, and plan to have five gorgeous babies."

"Rigghhtt," I tease.

"So, he's a great kisser. That means sex is phenomenal, right?" She smirks.

I shrug, pursing my lips.

"C'mon," she challenges. "Throw me a bone." She giggles. "You've boned, so share."

"We haven't," I inform her. "We messed around the other night, but the storms interrupted us."

"Fuck!" She groans, understanding my fear of storms. "Wait. What does 'messed around' mean?"

Thank goodness the sound of the French doors opening disrupts our conversation. We turn, finding Tag striding towards us. I blush head to toe.

Tag

I can't help but think I'm interrupting an intimate conversation as I walk toward Kate and Emma on lounge chairs. Emma's face and neck are beet red. Surely the sight of me doesn't cause her to blush. *I wonder what they were talking about?*

"Tag," Kate cheers. "Just the man we were talking about."

I look to Emma; she squirms after Kate's confession. I raise an eyebrow, causing her to avert her eyes.

"Grab your trunks and join us," Kate invites flirting.

"I don't want to interrupt your girl time," I state, wanting nothing more than to pull Emma away with me.

Kate looks at her cell phone. "We've been in the sun too long," she states. "I think I'll head in. I'm going out with friends tonight."

Clearly they've talked, and she's letting Emma spend time with me. I'm not about to argue. I learned I can't go a day without spending time with her.

"What are your plans the rest of the day?" I ask Emma.

"I..." she stammers. "No plans. How about you?"

"Kate, will you be here for dinner?" I ask before she disappears into the house.

"I'm meeting the girls at nine," she answers.

"Emma and I are making family dinner tonight," I announce without asking Emma's permission. We've cooked before, so I assume she won't mind.

"I'll be there," Kate calls over her shoulder.

"Let's go grocery shopping," I suggest, extending my hand to Emma.

31

EMMA

The five of us scurry around the kitchen, preparing to eat. Barry fills water glasses for each place setting, Kate lays a napkin and utensils at each seat, and Tag places salad plates on top of our dinner plates. Bonnie and I carry the salad bowl, rice, and shrimp étouffée to the center of the table.

"Wow. This looks delicious," Kate claps, already seated in her place.

When all of our bottoms hit our chairs, Barry insists on us holding hands around the table as he says grace. My sinuses burn and I fight tears. It's a family tradition; one the three of them share and allow Tag and I to join in on. We are a family now. We are a weird group thrown into an unordinary living situation. Tag and I are misfits—no relatives—adopted into this loving family.

Tag catches my sniffle, squeezing my hand on the table between us. I believe I see understanding in his slight smile and soft green eyes.

Kate passes the salad to her right. Tag uses the tongs to fill his salad plate, then passes the bowl to me.

As we eat our salads, the table falls quiet. Too quiet. In quiet moments, my mind spirals. Now it spirals to meals in my past with

Dad and Mom. Dad never tasted a meal I made. He doesn't know of my abilities with food.

"So," Kate interrupts the silence between salad bites. "Tag, what are your plans for our Emma?"

I choke, surprised by her forwardness. Bonnie, ever the mother, reaches over, patting me on the back as I sputter for breath.

Next to me Tag chuckles.

"I'm serious," Kate prods, eyes honed in on Tag.

"You don't have to answer that," Barry informs him.

"It's okay," Tag chuckles. "We're taking it slow."

Kate rolls her eyes, pushing her empty salad plate to the side.

This sparks Bonnie to rise, gathering everyone's small plates. I hate that she thinks she has to work even at our family dinners. There's no way I'm letting her clean up the kitchen.

"Pass me your plates; I'll serve the étouffée from here. The pot's still hot," Bonnie explains, standing at the head of the table beside her chair.

Obedient, we pass our plates, passing the full ones back to each other.

"Now," Kate continues.

I worry for Tag. She's forward, verbal, and a take-no-prisoners kind of girl.

"Emma, what are your intentions with our Tag?"

Okay, I didn't see that coming. Targeting me now is not at all what I expected.

"Um..." I nervously look to Tag, then Bonnie and Barry.

When I look back to Kate, she's giddy. She's loving my discomfort.

"It's hard to put into words," I explain.

"Kate, that's enough," her father warns.

"We are all invested in the going-ons in this house," she debates. "This thing between the two of them," she points her index finger between Tag and me. "If it goes south, it will have ramifications. And that will affect everyone in this house."

She's right.

"That's the reason we decided to take it slow," I inform all three of them. "All of you know that for three years the two of us barely spoke. Even though we share a house, it's like we are two strangers starting from scratch. It's scary as hell." My eyes dart to Tag, worried he won't understand what I mean.

"I've never felt this way. If it eases your mind, she's different and makes me want to be different," Tag swallows hard; I watch his Adam's apple bob. "I mean, she encouraged me to follow my passion; she's the reason I work less at the firm and more in a new area that interests me."

My insides warm at his words. He's proud of himself and enjoys the work he does now. I helped him realize that goal. My mom often told me, "You can't change a guy, so don't even try." I didn't try to change him; I simply told him what I observed and asked if he was truly happy. He made the decision; he made the change.

"She makes me want to be more," Tag confesses, barely more than a murmur.

With that confession, the room grows quiet again. Barry and Bonnie smile proudly, while Kate feigns disinterest. As I eat, my eyes often dart from Kate, to Barry and Bonnie. I wonder how they feel about Tag and my words. Bonnie expressed her support from the beginning. *I wonder if she still thinks it's a good idea.* Kate wanted all of the details, so I assume she likes the idea of my dating Tag. It's Barry that I can't read.

Tag sneaks his right hand under the table, placing it on my thigh, giving it a gentle squeeze. His support is appreciated. It keeps my mind from spiraling with worry over the thoughts of everyone at the table.

"So Kate, what are your plans for the night?" Tag challenges her to answer a tough question in front of her parents, like she did the two of us.

Kate shakes her head. She doesn't make eye contact; she doesn't speak a word. She just shakes her head, filling her mouth with more food. I fight my laughter at her discomfort. I must admit I enjoy her squirming like a worm for the tough questions she tossed at us with ease.

"You kids," Bonnie chuckles.

I love that she considers three adults as kids at the table, under her wing, and in our house.

"Emma you outdid yourself," Barry compliments, patting his spare tire of a belly.

"Hey, I helped," Tag chides.

"Yes, you did," I affirm.

"I cut up the lettuce, peppers, celery, and onions," Tag brags.

"And you did a fine job," I commend, patting his hand on the table between us.

"The entire meal was perfect," Bonnie states. "We should make this a weekly event."

"I like that," I state.

"I'd be up for that," Tag agrees. "Maybe Emma will allow me to do more than chop things."

Our family laughs as we clear the table as a team.

32

TAG

Pans clean and dishwasher running, Emma finishes wiping down the countertop while I wipe off the table. The domestic-ness of our meal does not escape me. I never experienced parents and children sharing a meal. Emma has, and I'm sure she misses it. I love that our new family unit made tonight special for her. Even better, Bonnie's suggestion that we do this every week will ensure Emma will experience family time.

"What shall we do with the rest of our evening?" I ask, ready to have her all to myself.

Emma shrugs. "What would you like to do?"

Hmm. What to do? What to do? I'd really rather her choose. I have an overwhelming desire to make her happy at all times.

"I like to walk at night," I admit.

"Me too," Emma confesses.

"Let's go for a walk," I suggest. I grab a bottle of water in case our walk lasts a long time, then follow Emma out the door.

We walk for several minutes, talking about birds, bunnies, and dogs we see along the trail. When a boy whizzes by rudely on his bicycle, I wrap my arms around Emma tugging her close to me to prevent him knocking her down. My heart races at light speed, my pulse pounding loudly in my ears. Though it wasn't a life-or-death situation, she would have sustained injuries if I hadn't pulled her off the path. The boy approached us at a rapid speed from behind. I hold her tight to my chest, my lips press firmly to her temple. Try as I might, I can't slow my breathing or my trembling hands.

"Motherfucker," I growl, my mouth to her skin. "Someone needs to teach that little shit some manners."

"I'm okay," Emma promises. "He's just a boy being a boy."

I hate to think what might have happened if I hadn't heard him speeding towards us from behind. Worst case scenario, he hurts Emma; best case scenario, he hurts himself. I press another kiss to her temple, urging her pulse to slow mine. I loosen my grip, my hands on her shoulders, holding her at arm's length. I scan her from head to toe and back, needing to see for myself she is not hurt.

"I'm okay," she states, a sweet smile upon her lips and her eyes tender.

"Prove it," I challenge, my nerves still on high alert.

Emma closes the distance between us, rises on her tiptoes, and covers my mouth with hers. She slowly opens and closes her lips over mine, willing mine to react.

Her lips work her magic, pulling me from my adrenaline high. I open my lips, pressing them softly to hers. Happy, I engage with her; I feel her smile as we kiss. I keep my lips soft, exploring her and the corners of her mouth.

Emma darts her tongue out, grazing mine in invitation. I move us farther from the walking trail as I tickle her tongue with mine. I moan out loud when she playfully closes her lips around my tongue, sucking it tightly. I mentally assess the area, trying to remember if a secluded spot is near.

I groan, breaking our kiss at the sound of approaching voices. Emma's eyes remain closed, and her right hand presses to her lips.

"C'mon," I urge her, hand to the small of her back. We return to the path, continuing our evening walk.

"I'm suddenly not in the mood to walk," Emma announces, looking up to me through her lashes. "Let's hang out at home instead."

I like her train of thought; privacy at home leads to more kisses without interruptions. We walk home at a quicker pace than we left, clearly we're both in a hurry to pick up where our kiss left off.

Emma

I berate myself with every step. *Where did the brazen, sex-starved woman come from that suggested we head home and make out?* I only know she woke up the night Tag settled his mouth between my thighs. Since then, sex consumes my mind twenty-four seven. There's something about Tag that calls to every part of me, and his talented lips kiss and suck emotions from me like no guy ever has before.

Stepping into the kitchen, my nerves ramp up to high gear. We tend to hang in the media room, but I'm not eager to revisit the scene of my storm freak out the other night, and our bedrooms will set the expectation of sex. Although I'm eager to explore more with Tag in that department, I don't want to rush things.

"First, snacks," Tag suggests, and I gladly follow his lead. "What will it be?"

"Chips," I suggest. "And something sweet."

I search the pantry shelf by shelf. I feel Tag's body heat before his chest connects with my back, and his arms reach around me, snagging a bag of peanut M&Ms.

"Perfect," I state, impressed with his choice of sweets.

I close the pantry door, but Tag doesn't move away. I turn my head, looking up over my shoulder. Goosebumps prickle my skin at the look in his sultry eyes.

"Wanna hang out in the library, or watch tv in your room?" He asks, his voice husky.

There's no television in the library and the furniture isn't the most comfortable. That leaves the media room or the sitting area in one of our bedrooms. His bedroom brings back memories from Friday night, causing my cheeks to heat. Maybe we'd be safer in my room.

"I'll behave," he vows, a sexy smirk swimming upon his lips.

What if I don't want him to behave? I mean, I'm game for some misbehaving. It's not misbehaving if we're both willing adults, right?

"I have some drinks in my mini fridge," I inform him, an open invitation to join me in my room.

His tongue quickly darts out to wet his lower lip and disappears. It's fast enough, I sort of wonder if I imagined it. He nods, backing away, his smirk still in place. Chips in hand, I head to my room with Tag close on my heels.

33

TAG

Emma places a hand on her door frame, looking toward me over her shoulder, her lower lip between her teeth. Still in her bikini from earlier, a thin t-shirt and Jean shorts mold wonderfully to her curves. She moves forward, willing me to follow her like prey into her lair. The phrase "willing victim" comes to mind. I will follow her anywhere.

"Make yourself at home," she invites, swinging her arm toward the overstuffed sofa in her seating area. She turns on the nearby lamp, then fetches the remote from her bedside table.

I place the chips and peanut M&Ms on the table before I situate myself at the end of the sofa, leaning against the arm. I track Emma's movements as she grabs a pillow from her bed before joining me. She sits beside me, pillow in her lap, pointing the remote toward the flat screen tv mounted on the wall.

"What shall we watch?" She asks, flipping through the channels.

"You choose," I answer, having no desire to watch television.

She clicks on the comedy heading, scrolling through movie after movie. My eyes are on her, so I don't see which movie she chooses.

"Which snack would you like first?" I ask, ready to pass her one.

When her cheeks pink, I know she's thinking of me as a snack. *I like the way she thinks.* I toss the pillow from her lap to the opposite end of the sofa, then tug her onto my lap.

She straddles me, her hands find my shoulders, and her pelvis perfectly aligns with mine. She wastes no time, leaning in, pressing her mouth to mine.

We feast on each other, all lips and tongues. Occasionally our teeth bump in our frantic need for one another. We kiss until we must pull away, gasping for breath.

I tuck her hair behind her ears and caress her cheeks, my need to touch her is strong. I watch her worry her lip as she seems to contemplate something.

"I'd like to try something," she murmurs, self-doubt washing over her.

How could I say no? I can't deny her anything. I nod, words escaping me. I'm not sure what to think when she closes her eyes for a moment, drawing in an audible breath.

She kisses my jaw, my neck, then tugs the hem of my shirt. Taking her hint, I remove my shirt, and she continues kissing my shoulder down to my chest.

Wait. Is she...? I replay her words in my mind. "I'd like to try something." *Try something as in something she's never done this before?*

"Emma," I barely recognize my husky voice. "You don't have..."

Lips hovering over my abs, her blue eyes dart up to my face. "I want to," she states with conviction.

A smile glides upon her lips before she presses them to me once again. She kisses and licks down my abs, around my navel, while trailing her fingers over my devil's trail.

I close my eyes, leaning my head on the back of the sofa. She has no idea the effect she has on me. She moves her mouth over me with bravado. It's sexy, this confidence towards her set task, a task she's confessed will be a first for her. When she sets her mind on something, she's virtually unstoppable. I gladly reap rewards from this.

When her fingertips move to my belt, I raise my head, my eyes meeting hers. Her fingers fumble, so I take over. I unbuckle my belt, then unfasten the button of my shorts. Before my hands move to my hips to slide my clothes off, she swats my hands away. I shake my head, smiling.

Emma teases the waistband of my boxer briefs with her fingers, her lips parted. Her warm breaths tickle the skin below my navel. Anticipation kills me; it's a sweet pain I'll gladly endure.

She sits further back on her knees, eyes locked on mine, as she slowly slides her hand under the fabric. Her palm grazes my sensitive skin as it sinks south. When her hand connects with my erection, her pupils dilate and her lips part. Sensing her apprehension, perhaps even fear, I grab her wrist.

"You don't have to…" I murmur.

Her tongue darts out, gliding over her lower lip. "Tell me how to," she whispers.

I shake my head. *She's not ready for this; we're moving too fast.*

She pulls her eyes from mine. With both hands, she lifts the waistband of my underwear over my swollen cock. At first sight, a gasp escapes her mouth. I watch her throat bob as she swallows her nerves. Her eyes dart to mine briefly before she gently kisses the tip. She startles when my cock twitches towards her. I fight my chuckle. Not deterred, she parts her lips slightly, kissing her way around the tip; her confidence grows with each point of contact. When she darts her tongue out, sliding it in a circle, then down my shaft, my head falls backward and a soft moan escapes.

"Is this okay?" she whispers, her lips grazing.

"Perfect," I encourage in a long, drawn-out groan.

At my confirmation, she continues exploring my shaft with light kisses and long licks. The combination of her warm tongue and gentle breaths stokes my inner fire. This woman will be the death of me.

When she reaches the base of my shaft, I feel the pads of her fingertips begin their exploration. She's hesitant, overly gentle, and not sure how to handle this part of me. I place my hand upon hers, encouraging her to wrap her long, slender fingers around my shaft. I urge her to stroke up, then down repeatedly.

In her eyes, I witness her delight in the power she wields in the palm of her hand. Emma enjoys eliciting a reaction from me; she comes alive with power.

Still stroking, she presses her lips to my tip. This time she opens her mouth, wrapping her lips around my shaft. Her warm, soft lips tighten as she hollows out her cheeks, sucking as much of me as she can, while her fist slowly pumps from my base.

I've been sucked off many times, never has it felt this overwhelming. With Emma, every sensation is magnified, each experience as if it's a first. In record time, my balls tighten, signaling my impending release.

"Em," I whisper. "Honey," I rasp. I place my hands on either side of her head, urging her off my cock. "I'm going to cum," I warn.

Emma's mouth engulfs more of me; I feel my tip against the back of her throat. Her fist remains wrapped around the bottom of my shaft when sparks shoot down my spine. My orgasm hits me like a tsunami. Her ministrations milk every last drop from me. I shudder from head to toe, my body tight.

Slowly, her grasp loosens and she places one more kiss to the head of my cock before settling back on her calves, eyes searching mine. I do my best to move the heavy lids covering most of my eyes. My hands urge her shoulders up onto me. She takes the hint, sitting on my lap, placing her palms upon my pecs.

"How'd I do?" she murmurs nervously.

"I came in record time," I'm embarrassed to state.

Her eyes seek affirmation in mine. She leans in, her lips press to mine. I channel my sincere thanks into our kiss; willing her to understand how amazing she is.

Emma rises from my lap, walking over to the top drawer of her nightstand. I tuck myself back into my pants, and I'm buttoning them when she returns with something in her hands, behind her back.

"I went to the doctor Monday," she confesses. "I started on birth control. It won't take effect until next week, but they gave me this in the meantime."

She waves a condom wrapper in her hand. I quirk my head, smirking. She tosses the condom on the sofa cushion beside me, returning to my lap. I freeze my lips upon hers when she starts grinding against me.

"Em…" I warn to no avail.

She moves her lips to my neck beneath my ear, her hips still moving. I place my hands on her hips, holding her in place.

"Emma," I warn, again. It takes every ounce of strength I have to hold myself back. "Slow, remember?"

"Screw slow," Emma retorts.

I want to chuckle; I want to throw caution to the wind. I want her —every piece of her.

"You're not ready. I don't want to hurt you," I explain.

"Hurt me?" She asks.

"You're so tight," I argue.

"I am not a virgin," she declares. "I can handle you."

"But I'm…"

"I think I can handle this." She cups my cock. "I have a large vibrator," she announces.

Did I hear that right? Sweet little Emma has a giant vibrator? She climbs from my lap, hands on her hips in challenge.

"Show me," I dare.

I follow her to the bottom nightstand drawer. She pulls it open, removes a lid from a decorative box, grasping the contents inside. She stands a toy in each hand, staring at the blue one in her right hand.

"I…" she stammers. "I guess it seemed big until I… um…" She looks towards my groin.

It's cute; she's cute. Until moments ago, she was proud of her large toy. Now, she realizes there are much bigger cocks in the world.

"Hop on the bed," I order, taking the vibrators from her hands.

She doesn't argue; she believes I'll give in to what she wants. I'll give her an orgasm or two, but I don't think she's ready for me. I place the toys on the table before I place my thumbs in the sides of her bikini bottoms, sliding them down her long, toned legs.

I kiss my way back up her body. Goosebumps appear the higher I climb up her thighs. I don't stop where she hoped, instead tugging her t-shirt up over her head. Eager, she unclasps her bathing suit top behind her back, and I slide the straps from her shoulders, down her arms, tossing it behind me.

I marvel at the naked woman spread on the bed before me. A large part of me wants to feast on her, fuck her for hours, then fall asleep in each other's arms.

Soon. Very soon, I will have her. I will give her all of me. In small ways, everyday, she's claiming more and more of my heart.

I nibble on her neck before kissing her long and hard. I sneak my hand to her nightstand. I smile devilishly as I kiss her, feeling for the larger of her two vibrators.

My thumb fumbles as I attempt to press the power button. Gentle humming fills the air when I am successful. I lay it on Emma's thigh, gently trailing it north. Emma's lips to mine, she mews in pleasure. I bring it over her hip, across her abdomen, and over her nipple. Vibration to her breast causes her to squirm.

"Hold still," I growl against her lips.

Instantly her wiggles cease. I move my mouth to her neck, nibbling and sucking as my right hand guides the blue vibrator to the apex of her thighs.

"Tag," she moans when the vibrator connects with her clit.

I suck gently on her pebbled nipple as I rub the vibrator through her folds.

"Open for me," I order before pulling her other nipple into my mouth, gently grazing my teeth over it.

I maneuver the vibrator through her slickness, allowing her to coat every inch of it.

"Mm-hmm," she moans.

When I position it at her entrance, she gyrates her hips encouraging me onward. I'm careful to slowly slide the toy an inch at a time.

"Ahh!" Emma beats her fists into the mattress at her side.

Fully submerged, I tap the illuminated button. The device kicks into high gear; its muffled humming increases. I press the button again and the long tentacles begin vibrating on her sensitive clit.

"Tag... I'm..." she stammers.

"Cum for me," I command, gently thrusting her toy half an inch over and over.

Her hips move in time with my movements. She grinds harder and harder against my thrusts. Her back arches, and a long moan escapes. Her movements halt as her orgasm arrives. I cease my thrusts but allow the vibrations to continue.

In the faint moonlight, I watch the muscles of her thighs spasm and her abdomen clench. Gently, I turn off the vibrator. Emma breathes heavily as her muscles relax, and she floats from her orgasmic high. She rolls towards me with heavy eyes. Her palm to my jaw, she softly kisses the corner of my mouth. I wrap my arms around her and skim my fingertips over her back. I hold her as her breaths even out.

I love the feel of Emma in my arms, and her naked flesh pressed tight to me. I marvel at the beautiful sight of Emma's climax.

She has not moved. *Is she asleep?* I tip my head back but cannot see. Carefully, I pull my arm from beneath her. She stirs slightly, adjusting her head on the pillow. I contemplate staying. I would love nothing more than to hold her as we sleep. Thinking better of it, I exit her bed.

Standing, I stifle a groan as I adjust my erect cock within my shorts. *Soon I will be inside her like the toy was tonight.* My cock twitches at the delicious thought.

I grab the vibrator and walk into her bathroom. I carefully close the door so as not to wake Emma. Next, I turn on the light and gently clean her prized blue vibrator. I smirk, remembering her insistence that her toy was as big as me, and her face when she realized I am much larger.

Patting the blue silicon dry, lettering catches my eye. "Angel" the letters read below the power buttons. It is fitting Emma's toy is named angel.

Emma

. . .

Summer's morning sunlight wakes me once again. I groan as I roll towards my nightstand and my cell phone. I smile at the paper propped on top of it. I love my name written in Tag's handwriting. For a guy, his cursive is impressively legible.

I unfold the note and read.

Angel,

I enjoy watching you sleep; it's my new favorite hobby.
I'm busy all morning, and golfing after Kate leaves.
Make today a good one.
Can't wait to see you tonight.

Yours,
Tag

Angel? Where did he come up with that? The new moniker perplexes me. I reread the note before placing it in the top drawer of my desk with his previous note. If this becomes a habit, I'll need a special box for these keepsakes.

There's a spring in my step, heading for my morning shower. I freeze at the sight of my blue vibrator laying upon a hand towel. Tag must have cleaned it last night when I fell asleep. I pick it up, returning it to my drawer. When I lay it in the box, I notice its name below the power button. I smile, shaking my head. "Angel" *So that's where he got the idea to call me that. It will be our inside joke.*

34

EMMA

"I can't believe you will be gone for six months straight," I pout, hugging Kate in the driveway. "Send me tons of photos of food."

Kate laughs, holding me at arm's length. "You are so weird. I will send you pics of hot guys standing near food."

"You're there to study," Barry barks as a reminder to his daughter.

Kate rolls her eyes dramatically.

"Don't do anything I wouldn't do," Kate says after hugging Tag.

"So, anything goes," he teases.

Bonnie, Kate, and Barry climb into Tag's Suburban, on loan to them for their trip to the airport in Kansas City.

"You two have fun," Bonnie calls to Tag and I through her rolled down window.

"Drive careful," I wave.

"I have the urge to cancel golf," Tag grumbles, wrapping his arm around my back.

"I have tasks to do," I remind him, hoping he keeps his tee time with the men from the firm.

"Do me a favor," he smiles down at me as we step into the

garage. "When you shop for groceries, take the Lexus, my card, and fill the tank for me."

He thinks leading me to believe I'm helping him will trick me into driving his car. For the second time in two weeks, he's insisting I use his vehicle instead of Bonnie and Barry's. *I may drive it, but I will not allow him to buy me one.* It's senseless; I don't need to spend this much on a vehicle.

The sun begins sinking in the west when, with the cameras rolling, I begin prep and marinate tonight's Thai roasted chicken thighs. I'm removing silk from two ears of sweet corn when Tag peeks his head into the pool house. He points to the camera then places his index finger over his lips.

I shake my head. "Come on in," I invite. "I can edit out parts. How was golf?"

Tag rolls his eyes. "The partners talked business and puffed their cigars for 18 holes straight."

"Let me rephrase my question," I chuckle. "How did you golf?"

"Six over," he grins proudly.

"Nice."

"What's for dinner?" he inquires, dipping his finger into the marinade. "Yum! That is delicious." He points to the sauce. "How can I help?"

"Salad fixings are in the fridge," I inform. "The chicken needs to marinade for thirty minutes before we grill. Let's make our salads then relax by the pool until it's time to start the grill."

"Sounds great," Tag smiles.

Closing the dishwasher, Tag suggests, "Let's swim."

I chew on my lip. He keeps his swimsuit in the pool house, while I take mine to my bedroom in the main house.

"Give me a minute," I hedge.

Tag's hands grasp my hips, halting me in place. A lazy smirk upon his face, Tag suggests, "We could swim in our underwear."

After the shock wears off, I process the location of the property ensures privacy, the fence shields us, and we have the house to ourselves for the weekend. Excitement tingles in my veins.

"It's dark," he encourages. "We can keep the pool lights off."

I close my eyes, drawing in a long breath, and nod. Tag pulls me tight to his chest, kissing my forehead.

Tag removes his golf shirt, while I dip my toes in the cool water.

"We don't…"

I cut him off, shaking my head as I raise the hem of my t-shirt. I find Tag staring at my chest when I toss my shirt to the pool deck. Glancing down, I remember I wear a lacy pink bralette today. *If this catches his eye, wait until he sees the matching dainty, pink boy shorts.*

I purposely shimmy my hips as I lower my shorts, feeling his green eyes searing my skin. While Tag stares, standing still like a statue, I dive headfirst into the pool. When I surface, he is stepping from his shoes then slacks. I tread water near the diving board, admiring Tag's muscular body in the shadows.

"Ready or not, here I come," he calls before diving into the depths near me.

In the dark, I struggle to see him swimming beneath the surface. I expect him to pop up in front of me. Instead, I feel his fingers wrap around my ankle seconds before he tugs me under with him. He releases me immediately, and we surface face to face. I sputter a bit, playing up the fact he dunked me without warning.

"Not nice," I state, swatting his shoulder.

"I'm sorry," he drawls, wrapping his arms around my waist. "Will you ever forgive me?"

I shake my head, jutting out my lower lip to pretend pout.

"What can I do to make you forgive me?" his gravelly voice tickles my ear.

Goosebumps rise on my skin despite the summer heat.

Tag

Emma's tongue swiping across her lower lip, coupled with our proximity, sends my desire into overdrive. I need to put distance between us if I have any hope of taking it slow like Emma needs.

"Follow me," I murmur and swim to the shallows.

I take deep breaths as we work our way over. *I need to calm down.* I sit on the steps, stretching my legs and leaning back.

I can't help but notice the shape of her breasts, within her bra, water dripping and shining in the lights. *She is going to be the death of me.*

Emma looks at me expectantly. I lean my head back and look at the night sky. After a bit, she comes over, leaning her warm body against mine. We sit like this for a moment, enjoying the quiet night.

"What are you thinking about?" she asks.

"I am not sure," I respond. I mean it. My thoughts have been racing recently. I always have so much to think about between work, Emma, and the other stressors of day-to-day life. "How about you?"

She pauses a moment before responding. "I am thinking about the future."

"What about it?"

"You." She kisses my cheek. "The restaurant. What to make for my next video." She goes quiet.

"What else?" I ask, turning to look at her. I am enamored by her beauty under the starlight. Her hair is wet and messy, her eyes reflect the starlight, and her soft smile makes me want to kiss her.

"Us. What we are becoming?" She searches my eyes for a moment, trying to gauge what I feel. "I'm... still scared." She looks away.

I pull her closer to me, grabbing her chin and lifting it, looking deep into her blue eyes.

"It's okay if you are scared. I am scared, too. Being scared is a part of life." I pause to think, struggling to find the right words. "I was scared to change how I lived my life. Sometimes fear follows the right decisions, I think."

I look at her, I can tell she is contemplating what I have said. I continue, "As always, I still want to take things slow. I… know you have been hurt. I don't want to hurt you."

She pulls away from me a bit when she hears this. *Did I do something wrong? I didn't mean to upset her.*

Emma

I find pain in Tag's eyes. *He knows.* Bile coats my throat, and a burning sensation broils in my belly. *Bonnie must have told him.* I can't be mad at her. After the hell I put him through that night, he deserves to know.

He will never look at me the same again. I will forever be damaged. I don't want or need his pity; I need friendship. I chew on the inside of my cheek as I scoot away from him, water sloshing around me.

I need a moment to breathe. I don't like thinking about it. Part of me starts to panic, flashbacks playing through my head. I get up to get out of the pool, quickly walking over to where my clothes are and scooping them up.

"Emma?" I hear Tag call behind me. I don't look back. I can't. Tears are beginning to well in my eyes. I don't want him to see me as "damaged goods". *I didn't want him to know.* I don't want to talk about it or think about it.

"Emma, stop for a second," Tag pleads, his voice full of pain.

I stop, but I can't bring myself to look at him.

"I'm sorry that happened to you," he shares, his voice breaking. "I wish I had been here to help. The things I want to do to those boys…" He pauses, taking a deep breath. "You didn't deserve that. I should have been there to defend you. I should have been there helping you through every storm that passed, but now I can help you through all the ones that will come in our future. I want to keep you safe from now on."

I look at him now, his hair dripping onto his bare shoulders, his skin shining in the moonlight, his chest rising and falling, and his green eyes, so sad and full of love. *He means it.*

"I don't want your pity," I say, shaking. "I am not broken or fragile. Everyone else looks at me that way." My voice breaks as I start to sob. "Bonnie and Barry treat me like a tea cup. Now you are going to see me like that as well."

He closes the distance between us, hugging me to his chest.

"You are the strongest woman I know, Emma." His voice vibrates through his chest, low and calming.

My tears are slow.

Tag

Emma's pain guts me. I rub her shoulder as I hold her. We stand like this for a few moments as her breathing slowly calms down.

"Let's go get you warm," I say when I realize she trembles.

She nods and sniffles as she stands up tall again, trying to compose herself. I lead her upstairs to her room.

"No." She stops. "I want to be with you tonight," she whispers, her eyes looking up at me.

I nod, changing directions. I am equal parts nervous and excited as I close my bedroom door behind us. I contemplate towels versus a warm shower. Noticing Emma's shivers, I guide her to my shower. I turn the shower spray to warm, before removing my boxers.

Emma stands frozen in place, eyes on the tile beneath her feet.

"Can I?" I ask, gesturing at her wet underwear.

She nods.

Gently, I pull down her wet bottoms then lift her bra over her head. I do not think of sex; instead, I want to protect her, I want to hold her, and I want to keep her warm.

Under the warm shower spray, I hold Emma to my chest. Eventually, she looks up to me through her wet lashes.

"I am okay." She emphasizes each word.

"I know you are. You are amazing and strong." I squirt shampoo into each of our palms. "I needed you to know Bonnie told me the day after the storm. You are not damaged. You survived. Everyone has a weakness—storms are yours."

We rinse our hair then take turns slathering each other with slippery body wash. Emma's worries seem to fade as her giggles echo off the enclosed shower walls.

Clean, I turn off the shower and grab a towel from the warming rack, gently wrapping it around her. She closes her eyes, leaning against me. Sensing she wants me to dry her, I slowly continue my way down her entire body. I am infatuated with her beauty and comfort in her own skin. Standing back up, I place a gentle kiss on her forehead.

I softly push her shoulders toward the door. "Go lay down under the blankets, I will join you in a moment."

As I quickly dry myself off, I Mentally prepare myself for a night with Emma wrapped in my arms. *Slow. Take it slow.*

35

TAG

Head on my pillows, Emma's naked body splays on the bed. Like her breasts, she is real from head to toe. The woman definitely worships food, it is part of her job, but her daily swims and runs keep her tone.

Lying beside her, distracted by her beauty, I trail my fingertips along her ribs, causing her to wiggle to escape. I forgot she is ticklish.

"Hold still," I scold.

"It tickles," she laughs.

"Would you prefer pain?" I tease.

Fear engulfs her wide eyes.

"Teasing," I chuckle. "I was teasing."

I must be careful not to scare her from my bed. She is skittish. She has been hurt in the past. I need to prove she can trust me.

I walk my fingers over her abdomen, focusing my attention between her thighs. Emma's hand clutches my wrist, halting my progress.

"I want you in me," she murmurs.

I place a peck to the corner of her mouth as I guide her hand to my erect cock. Her touch brings a rasp to my voice. "I need you ready before I can bury myself."

"Oh, I am ready," she moans, as my fingers delve between her thighs.

I dip one long finger within her, imagining her hot, wet walls surrounding my more-than-ready cock. On my next thrust, I add a' second finger, slowly stretching her. I am the luckiest man alive with Emma in my bed, nothing between our bodies.

The sound she emits is the same one she makes when she enjoys food. *Great. Now her sounds while eating will forever remind me of our time in my bedroom.*

My thoughts back on my actions, I concentrate on my fingers thrusting within her and add a scissoring motion, encouraging her to expand for me. Emma turns onto her side, her grip on my cock more fervent. The heady sensation is more than I can take.

"Condom," I rasp.

"Uh-huh," she protests, not loosening her grip. "My shot has taken effect. We're safe."

No condom. I fight the urge to pounce upon her, burying myself balls deep in one massive thrust.

"Eeemmmaaa!" a female voice calls through the house.

In unison, Emma and my heads turn to the open bedroom door. With Bonnie's family in Kansas City, we were supposed to have the house to ourselves tonight.

"Rachel," Emma whispers, disengaging her hand, and darting from my bed.

I am frozen in place, watching her scramble to my dresser for a shirt and shorts.

"Stay here," she murmurs before slipping out the door, shutting it behind her.

"Argh!" I groan, flopping onto my back. My arm covers my eyes. I cannot will my erection to fade, so I climb from my bed. I pout as I turn on the shower. My hand is not what I planned to enjoy tonight.

36

EMMA

Rachel stands in the foyer, arms hugging her stomach, calling my name. She looks lost, scanning the large house for help. I wonder why she didn't just walk up to my bedroom but am grateful she didn't climb the stairs. As I descend the staircase, I notice her red face and puffy eyes.

"Rach... what's wrong?" I greet as I approach with outstretched arms.

Loud sobs fill the air as I embrace my best friend. I struggle to understand her. All I make out is, "Where's Tag?"

I hold her at arm's length. "I'm not sure, let's go to my room," I offer.

I assist my friend up the stairs, turning her in the opposite direction of Tag's corridor. She flops on my bed, clutching a pillow to her chest.

I keep my voice low. "Rachel, honey, talk to me."

Her sobs grow louder. "We...we...he..."

Oh no. Justin must have dumped her.

"He... we didn't use... condom."

I jerk. Not at all what I expected. Rachel often cries when her whirlwind relationships end, however never as bad as this. This is much worse than her emotional turmoil after falling headfirst for a guy.

"So…you had sex without…" My chest aches as I try to say the words out loud.

Rachel nods amid loud sobs. I fear my pillow will look like I threw it in the pool before the night is over. I take a moment to collect my thoughts. *Unprotected sex…Chance of pregnancy…*

"When was your last period?" I ask, needing to cut to the specifics.

"A…a week or two ago," she says with hiccupping sobs.

Crap. I cannot lie to her. The timeline sucks.

"So, this is not the best time to forget," I think out loud. "Where's Justin?" *Why isn't he with her?*

"Poker night," she grumbles.

Did she just say poker night? I fight the urge to drift off on my own tirade at his selfishness. *I must put my opinions aside and support my friend.*

"Does he know you are upset?" I ask, needing to know how she got from his bedroom to searching frantically for me.

Rachel nods, her head against my comforter.

"Did you talk about this before he left?"

Again, she nods. "We talked a minute before he had to leave."

Had to leave? HAD to leave? Focus. Support Rachel.

"He… he apologized," she hiccups. "He said he'd support my decisions."

How noble of him. So, if he supports her decisions, why is she with me and not him? I slip from my seat beside her on the bed to fetch her a water. *She's bound to be dehydrated from all her tears.*

"Drink," I encourage, holding the open water bottle to her mouth.

I watch as she sits up in super slow motion, takes a minuscule sip, then returns to the fetal position. *This may be a long night.*

37

TAG

ME

up?

I stare at my cell phone, anxious for Emma's reply. Several minutes pass before someone taps their finger lightly three times against my door.

"Yeah?" I call.

Emma catches me off guard by opening the door wide and stepping inside. I ensure the sheet covers my waist as I am naked in my bed.

"Hey, How's Rachel?" I ask.

"Asleep for now," Emma responds, standing near the door.

"Everything okay?" I inquire, sensing there is something more.

She nods. "She will be, she needed to talk some things through."

"About Justin?" I ask.

Emma Nods.

"He's at poker," we say in unison and chuckle.

Emma walks from one window to another, pausing to look down to the pool out back.

"Is it bad?" I question, needing to understand her mood.

"No. It's not even anything for certain. She's just worried." Emma brushes it off.

"Anything I can do?"

"Is he a good guy?" she asks, now facing me with arms crossed over her chest.

"Justin?" I query, struggling to follow her.

She nods.

"Yeah, he is," I answer, needing to put her fears to rest on this topic once and for all. I share, "He dated his high school girlfriend for three years into college. He's had two other steady girlfriends since then." I take a deep breath. "He's had bad luck, though. The one from high school, took a semester abroad her junior year of college, then opted not to return to the States. The other two women cheated on him."

Emma

Great. Let's hope Justin has better luck now for Rachel's sake. If not, she will be pregnant.

"Did he hurt her?" Tag asks, concerned.

I shake my head. "I can't tell you more than that. It's not my story to tell."

Tag scoots to the edge of the bed as he reaches his arm towards me. When he shifts the sheet falls, exposing his bare hip. I gasp, my eyes wide, and dart to the door as Tag pulls the sheet back into place.

"Goodnight," I call, waving over my shoulder.

Tag

Spooked. Emma is spooked, and I'm naked. So, I can't chase after her.

I toss and turn; there is no way I will fall asleep tonight. *Why did she run? What about me scared her? I'm trying to go slow.*

I snag my cell phone from my nightstand.

> ME
>
> What did I do?

I watch the eclipse, waiting for her response.

> EMMA
>
> needed to get back in case she woke up

Again, I watch the little blue dots, but no message comes.

> ME
>
> you looked scared

Anxious to hear from her, another long pause, frustrates me.

> EMMA
>
> do u always sleep naked?

I chuckle. She ran at the sight of my bare hip. A wide smile takes residence upon my face. Emma ran, but she's curious.

> ME
>
> naked or PJs
>
> find out for yourself

> EMMA
>
> stop

> ME
>
> can't divulge all my secrets
>
> you'll grow bored with me

Once more, I stare at the dots, willing her to reply.

> EMMA
>
> c u @ breakfast

> ME
>
> goodnight

I laugh out loud at the thought of Emma in her bed, thinking of me naked under my covers. *Definitely no way I'm gonna sleep. I need to go rub one out in the shower.* I shake my head. *I will not be the guy who masturbates twice in less than three hours with thoughts of the woman down the hall.*

I throw off the sheet, leave my phone on the bed, and head to the pool. *Laps. Laps until I am unable to walk.* That is what I need to allow me to fall asleep. *I wonder if Emma struggles clearing her mind to find sleep.*

38

EMMA

Rachel and I barely say a word as we eat breakfast the next morning. I slept less than five hours as thoughts of Tag sleeping naked haunted my mind.

"What time do you get off work?" Tag asks Rachel, entering the kitchen. When she answers at three, he suggests, "You two should join Emma and I for our four o'clock tee time at the club." He looks from Rachel to me and back. "You're done at the shelter by then, right?"

I nod. Rachel states she'll consider it and leaves it at that. With protein shake in hand, Tag leaves the kitchen as quick as he entered. Rachel points her index finger at his back as he leaves the room, then mimics a cock jutting in and out of her mouth. I shake my head, and she cranes her neck, ensuring he's out of earshot.

"Don't lie to me," she chides. "I'd have to be blind not to see the way he acts near you. Check that. Even then I would feel it in the air." She leans across the kitchen island towards me. "So, when did the two of you finally hook up?"

Again, I shake my head.

"Stop it," she squeals. "I tell you everything."

"You tell me too much sometimes," I tease.

"Spill," Rachel orders, then looks at her watch. "I have to leave in five minutes." She fake pouts.

"We've been talking that's all," I inform.

She gives me a pointed look. "And you kiss. You practically swoon when he's in the room."

"I do not," I protest.

"So…" she draws out. "Will there be more kissing and stuff?"

If I told her what she interrupted last night, she would feel like a heel and I do not want that. She needed me, I want to be there for her like she's always been there for me.

"I better go so the two of you can have the entire house to yourselves." She wiggles her eyebrows suggestively.

"Go!" I order, chucking and point to the door.

39

TAG

Emma looks good in golf attire. Her black shorts are a perfect length —short enough to tastefully display her long toned legs and slightly snug to show her curves. Her collared, sleeveless golf shirt hides perfect breasts that I have only begun to worship. Her narrow waist, shirt tucked into her shorts, and a black belt create a slender perfect hourglass figure. She is picture perfect in her matching golf shoes and visor. Emma now has all my attention, and I cannot stop thinking about her. My world is alive for the first time, and she is the reason.

Justin interrupts my drooling over Emma. "I fucked up," he confesses as the cart darts down the path. "I forgot to put on a condom." Justin rubs the palms of his hands into his eyes.

"FFuucckk," I drawl.

"I got so wrapped up in her, in how good…" he groans, shaking his head. "Has a woman ever had that effect on you?" He looks to me.

I shake my head, unable to speak. My feelings for Emma grow stronger every day, and we've only begun. I can only imagine the flood of senses and emotions she will stir within me. I close my eyes tight.

It all makes sense now. The reason Rachel came over so upset, then Emma's reaction in my bedroom to my bare skin. The real ramifications of sex and its consequences are front and center in her mind.

"I shouldn't have gone to poker," he states. "I rushed out, when I should have stayed and had an important conversation with Rachel."

I nod, remembering Rachel's puffy face, red eyes, and tears when she arrived. She needed him. Until now, a pregnancy scare was only a couple of days in my mind. Our friends now have three weeks or more to worry.

I park our cart, and waste no time choosing my next club.

"Come here," I demand, pulling Emma by the arm, tight to my chest. "Justin just told me everything," I murmur.

She leans against me. "They talked it all out today," she whispers.

"He says they're no longer fighting," I restate what Justin shared with me.

I feel her cheek move against my chest as she nods.

"I'm glad you were there for her." I squeeze her tight before releasing her. "Slow is good," I whisper, eyes locked on hers.

Nodding, she parrots, "Slow is good."

Wanting to lighten the mood again, I devise a plan. I take two steps back.

"Care to make a wager?" I taunt, loud enough for others to hear.

Emma's eyes spark to life at my challenge.

"If you outdrive me on this hole," I start. "I'll do anything you ask me to for an entire week."

"Anything?"

"Anything," I restate. "Justin and Rachel are my witnesses."

"And if you out drive me?" Emma inquires, head tilted to the side and hands upon her hips.

"You will let me buy you a new vehicle, without argument," I announce.

Her mouth opens, closes, opens, then closes again. She already wants to argue about the car. I'm proud that my challenge causes her to pause. I might just get my way after battling her for years.

"It's a win-win for you," Rachel tells her. "You can't lose."

"In or out?" I challenge.

"In!" She blurts loudly.

I motion for her to tee off first, but she shakes her head.

"You first, I insist," she orders, swinging her hand in the direction of the men's tee box.

I will give her this victory, as I intend to win our bet. I approach the tee box, my seven wood in hand. I send my tee shot soaring down the center of the fairway, then sweep my arms wide in a half bow, offering the tee box to Justin.

Emma

I park our cart near Tag's drive instead of driving on down to mine. I bite my lips tight between my teeth, fighting the urge to gloat. Both Justin and Tag place their second shots on the green before walking back to their cart. Tag drives the men's cart behind ours to first Rachel and then my ball in the fairway. I hit an easy nine iron, setting my ball on the front edge of the green.

Having refrained from commenting on my tee shot out-driving his, Tag stands at the back of our cart when I return. I drop my iron into my bag seconds before he wraps his arm around my lower back, pulling my firmly against him. My hands grip his shoulders to steady myself. Molten green eyes pierce my soul as his mouth meets mine. Tag's hands cup my cheeks, his firm lips feast upon mine. His tongue heavy on my lower lip, I part for him. My knees grow weak, and my heart pounds rapidly. He leaves me breathless, frozen, and thirsty for more.

"Whoa, I didn't know…" Justin cheers. "When did the two of you become a couple?" He points his finger back and forth between us.

"I guess… right now," Tag answers, smiling widely at me. His lustful eyes search mine for any argument.

"It better be right now, or she lied to me, her best friend in the entire world, this morning," Rachel teases.

"I didn't lie to you," I tell her. "I guess we are now officially a couple that demonstrates affection in public."

I glare at Tag, but it lacks full conviction.

"No one saw us," he tells me, scanning the surrounding area.

"We saw it," Rachel proudly states, raising her hand in the air.

I stick my tongue out at her, causing her to laugh before turning around in the golf cart seat.

"That's very mature," Tag murmurs, teasingly into my ear before placing sweet kiss on my exposed neck.

"We're golfing," I remind him, swatting playfully.

"Yeah, we're golfing," Justin parrots. "Can we get back to it, or do we need to let the two of you go home?"

"Yeah, yeah." Tag takes the driver's seat and drives toward the green.

I stand frozen in place for a moment.

"Emma," Rachel calls, stirring me from my shock.

"Did that really just happen?" I ask, following the men.

"Yep. A week ago we were two very single women, now we are in relationships with two hot, older guys," Rachel brags, waking up her cell phone. "Smile," She snaps a selfie of the two as we pull up to park. "We look blissfully happy, don't you think?"

I stare at my image. I do look happy. *I am happy.*

After the round, we find a four-top table on the patio of the club, where the guys order water for Rachel and I, beers for them, and appetizers. We've finished our first drink and ordered a second when Justin groans audibly.

"This can't be happening," he grumbles, looking to Tag.

"Brace yourselves; here comes Justin's parents," he warns, chuckling.

Rachel and my heads turn toward an older couple walking up the sidewalk from the putting greens. Justin's mom waves a broad smile upon her face. She's dressed in a black skort paired with a hot pink golf shirt. Her hat and socks match her shirt, while her shoes are black like the skort. She's tall and brown-haired like her son, but carries over thirty extra pounds on her frame.

"Hi guys," she greets, stopping within feet of our table. Her husband barely glances our way as he continues into the clubhouse.

Justin rises, places his hands upon her upper arms, kissing her on the cheek.

"Mom, I'd like you to meet, Rachel," he smiles warmly now standing behind her chair. "Rachel, this is my mother, Julie."

"Hi," Rachel waves, nervously. "This is my best friend, Emma."

"How'd the four of you golf?" she asks, her eyes scanning Rachel head to toe.

"The greens are fast, but we played well," Tag answers, his hand landing on my bare thigh under the table.

"Happy to hear," she states, glancing over her shoulder. "We're running late. Your father made us a tee time with the Kramers."

"Good luck," Rachel offers before stuffing a grilled Brussel sprout in her mouth.

"I need to fetch your dad," she states, waving. "I hope we'll see you again soon." Her eyes look to Rachel before she heads inside.

"Bathroom?" Rachel asks, already standing.

I nod, then scurry to follow her to the women's room door around the side of the building.

"I can't believe that just happened," she shares, fluffing her pony-tail at the vanity.

"You should feel good," I state. "He didn't hesitate to introduce you to his mother."

"RRiigghhtt," she draws out. "But he didn't introduce me as his girlfriend." Her eyes lock on mine in the mirror.

"And he didn't introduce you as a friend," I remind her. "Take the win. I'm sure you'll share a family dinner with them in the next couple of weeks."

"Like I need that added stress," Rachel whines.

"Stop," I chide. "Everything seemed okay between you on the course."

"Yeah, we talked for an hour this afternoon," she smiles. "He's willing to support me no matter what I decide."

Good. Tag's right, he is a good guy.

"And what have you decided?" I inquire.

She looks under each stall door, finding no one, she shares, "I don't want to take the morning after pill." She leans her bottom against the counter facing me. "So, we'll wait three weeks and see."

"And if you are pregnant?"

"I told him I'm not ready to get married," she shrugs, trying to make light of it. "He agrees if I am pregnant that we will co-parent and promises he'll support the baby and me."

I hug my best friend. "I'm here, too," I remind her.

Hours later, we stand in our driveway, waving as our two friends back out. It feels very adult-like standing near him after golfing and waving as our friends leave.

"Want a snack?" He asks, leading me inside.

"We split three apps at the club after golfing, I couldn't eat another bite. I'd rather have a beer," I inform him.

Tag guides me to the bar, my hand in his. He pulls two cold beers from the fridge, pops off the lids, laying them on the counter, and strides toward me. As I reach for a beer, he leans his head, his lips colliding with mine. I gasp, caught off guard, and he takes advantage of my parted lips, slipping his tongue inside. His hot tongue is heavy on mine, beside mine, under mine. Its heat warms my throat, flows down my chest, and pools deep in my belly.

My fists grip his shirt at his abdomen in hopes to anchor me to the ground as I feel I'm floating to the ceiling. His right hand grasps the nape of my neck while his left digs into my hip, holding me to him.

Time seems to stand still as we consume one another. When he pulls away, I'm left gripping him tightly as I gasp for breath. His liquid, green eyes see all of me, gazing into my soul.

"DDaammnn." He closes his eyes, shaking his head.

Damn? Damn what?

I thought it was the kiss to end all kisses, hot as hell, and life changing. *Is it possible that what I believed to be the perfect kiss wasn't earth shattering for him?*

Pulling myself together, I release my fists from his shirt and lean to my right to grab a beer bottle. My hand trembles as I raise the long neck to my lips. The cold beer feels sublime against my overheated throat, but I don't taste it.

I chance a quick glance, my eyes finding his locked on me. Caught in his tractor beam, I can't look away, I can't move. I'm a doe frozen in his high beams; my life in his hands.

Tag

"DDaammnn." I moan.

I close my eyes, shaking my head. *How can one kiss affect me so?* I've kissed a lot of women, a wide variety of ladies, and never felt half the emotion, the heat, the passion in this one kiss with Emma.

It kills me to think this beautiful woman lived under the same roof as me for over three years, and I'm only now realizing how great she is.

I can't pull my eyes from her mere inches from me. I should help her reach for her drink, I should say something, but all I can manage is a dumbfounded stare.

Snap out of it! I shake away my kiss-induced haze.

"Emma," I plead.

In her eyes I see… fear. *Why fear?*

"Hey," I coo, taking her chin in hand. "Too soon?" I ask, needing to know how I ruined our perfect moment.

She shakes her head, moving my hand with it.

I take one step back and then another. I need to put distance between us before I pull her to me, attempting to kiss away the worry I see on her face.

"I…" My voice cracks. "That kiss…" I struggle for words to share all that her kiss stirred within me. "I've never felt anything like it." Clearly words escape me.

Her eyes widen, hope sparking to life. "Really?"

"Didn't you feel it, too?" I urge.

She nods her head, a wide smile growing upon her face. "When you cursed, I was afraid you didn't feel…"

I interrupt her, "That wasn't a curse. That was praise. I had to step back so I wouldn't attack you right here on the bar." I move towards her, placing my palms flat on the bar top at her sides. Pinned in place, she can't escape. My lips an inch from hers I continue, "That kiss ignited an inferno in my veins, my heart's jack-hammering against my ribs, and I won't tell you how my cock reacted."

"The entire day's been foreplay," I state with a smirk. "Hell, you started pushing my buttons as we cooked dinner last night. You've wound me so tight I'm afraid I'll explode any second, embarrassing myself."

Her cheeks pink, and she giggles.

My lips brush hers as I tease, "I can't believe you thought I didn't enjoy our kiss."

I hover close, feeling her breath on my cheek, watching reactions flicker in her eyes. She presses her lips to mine, her fingers lacing in my hair, holding my mouth to hers. She is ravenous, feasting on my lips, and exploring every part of my mouth. Taking what she wants from me, she's jet fuel on my flames.

"Want to…" I tilt my head toward the door and the staircase beyond.

"Yes!"

At her answer, three things war within me. I long to lift her onto the bar and take her right here. I want to lift her over my shoulder, carrying her to my bed fireman-style. I should take her hand in mine, leading the way. I need her, every part of her, but I don't want to rush this thing between us. I feel as though my head might explode as the battle wages within.

Unable to wait another second, my body takes over. My hands at her hips, I lift her onto the pool table, her mouth still exploring mine. I move my palms to her cheeks, focusing on our kiss. Emma's hands untuck my golf polo from my slacks, and she slowly lifts its hem up my torso. Following her lead, I raise my arms over my head, and she breaks our kiss removing my shirt then tossing to the tile floor below.

Her eyes devour my chest and drool on my abs. Enjoying her reaction to my body, I smirk.

"My eyes are up here," I tease.

"Umm, sorry," she sputters, her eyes finding mine.

My smirk morphs into a genuine smile under her gaze. I nearly flinch when her fingertips connect with my bare chest. The warmth of her touch sends sparks straight to my heart. Her eyes follow her fingers as they slide down my pectorals. The zings continue when the pads of her fingers trace my ribs to my abdominals. Her gentle touch nearly brings me to orgasm. I'm reacting like a fourteen-year-old boy. *At this rate, I will blow my load the moment I remove my pants. Check that. I'm worse than a fourteen-year-old boy.*

"Kiss me," I beg.

Emma holds up one finger between us, pausing my approach. She lowers her hands between us, clutching the hem of her shirt.

"Let me," I insist, replacing her hands with mine.

Inch by inch, I slowly lift her shirt, my thumbs grazing her smooth skin as I uncover her beauty lying beneath. At her ribcage, she squirms.

"I'm ticklish," she reminds me through her giggle, and it's the sweetest sound in the world.

I vow to find every sensitive, ticklish spot she hopes to hide from me.

Emma

My skin prickles, exposed to the air-conditioned room. Seeking Tag's heat, and shelter from his lustful gaze, I slide my hands up his back, pulling him into me. Pressed chest to chest, I peer up through my lashes, imploring him to kiss me, to caress me, to hold me close and never let me go.

Lifting my chin, he closes the distance between us. First, I kiss one corner of his mouth, then playfully peck the other corner. Apparently, I take too long. Tag nips my bottom lip, gently tugging it between his teeth. I attempt to decipher the wicked glint in his eyes. I'm not sure if he's teasing me or challenging me to react.

When he releases my lower lip, I place a peck upon his cheek, then nuzzle his ear with my nose as I attempt to unfasten my bra behind my back. *Fuck! It's a sports bra. Damnit!* It's impossible to remove it without two hands and arm movements.

"Sorry," I excuse, pulling back while crossing my arms in preparation to remove it.

"Let me," he suggests, gently caressing the flesh near its lower band.

Licking his lower lip, eyes focused on the task at hand, he slips his fingers beneath, grazing my breasts before he lifts the fabric. His hands pause below my chin, his eyes fixated on my exposed breasts. Sensing his presence, my nipples pebble with his adoration.

"My eyes are up here," I parrot the phrase he tossed at me moments ago, snapping him from his worship.

He bends, sucking one hard nub between his hot lips as his hands extricate me, tossing the bra. His hands upon my back, he lavishes the other nipple as he did the first. My head falls back, and my chest arches towards him. The combination of wetness and his hot breaths nearly undoes me.

"TTaagg," I drawl, begging him to stop yet wanting more.

Rising, his heavy-lidded eyes smolder. He places the palm of his hand between my breasts, gently pressing, urging me to lie back upon the felt.

Tag drags his tongue toward my navel as his hands make quick work of my belt, button, and zipper. He licks, nips, and sucks along my waistband while he positions his hands at my hips, his thumbs hooked in my belt loops.

Leaning on my elbows, his eyes find mine through his long, dark lashes as his hands shimmy my shorts and panties from my hips, down my thighs. Inch by inch more warm flesh comes in contact with the cool air around me. The sensation nearly overloads my already heightened senses.

I long to squirm, feeling exposed beneath the bright pendant lighting, laid out before him. This is new territory for me; excitement and fear pulse through my veins.

"Tag," I whisper, starving for his touch.

"You're beautiful," he proclaims, eyes still scanning intimate parts of me.

"I'm not...," I stammer.

These words pierce his lust; they bring worry to his brow. "Too fast?" He asks, concerned.

I shake my head, lifting up to sit before him and biting my lip. "I don't have much experience," my voice breaks announcing my nerves.

He shakes his head. "That doesn't matter to me," he promises. "We can stop. We don't have to do anything you're not ready for."

His hands brush back stray hairs stuck to my sweaty face. He cups my head in his large hands, warmly searching my face for answers.

"I want to," I whisper huskily. "I need you."

"Yeah?" He seeks further permission.

My nod is all the permission he seeks. He boosts me from the table, hands cupping my ass. I wrap my legs around his waist and my arms around his neck. Mouth pressed to mine, tongues tango as he carries me to the stairs.

He pauses halfway up the staircase, pressing me to the wall, his forehead pressed to mine, his eyes closed, and his breath ragged. I give him this moment, my fingers twirling the long brown hair on the top of his head. Slowly, his eyes open. I've never seen such emotion. His break over, he carries me faster now. I giggle at our urgency down the corridor to his master suite.

Feeling the bump of his shins on the edge of the bed, I lower my legs to the mattress before removing my arms from his neck. Naked, I stand before him in the faint moonlight from the windows and the dim light of the hallway. He strikes a commanding pose. Bare chested, he's a dark shadow, with the light from the doorway framing him from behind.

"Lay down," he orders, and I immediately obey.

I walk back, positioning myself in the center of his enormous bed. I chew on my lip while my eyes follow his hands to the waistline of his slacks. I feel wetness pool between my thighs, and I ache as I watch him unfasten his pants slowly.

As if he knows the torture he subjects me to, he slowly slides his golf slacks from his thighs past his knees to pool at his feet. I stare awestruck at the gorgeous Adonis clad only in tight boxers before me. The man is a testament to power and beauty. He's tone but not overly bulky. His shoulders are broad from hours of swimming, his waist is slim, his thighs powerful, and don't get me started on the impressive bulge beneath his black boxer briefs.

He places his palms on the foot of the bed, his eyes locked on me like an apex predator. I squeak in anticipation, slapping my hand over my mouth. Slowly he crawls up the bed, hovering inches above my body. His magnetism strong, I force my body to remain in place instead of wrap around him.

He props himself on one elbow, planking above me. His free hand caresses my cheek as his mouth lowers to mine. His lips kiss, his mouth nips, and his tongue licks. My mouth returns the favor, while my hands softly brush back and forth over his ribcage.

When his mouth finds skin below my ear, my body arches, and my head turns, exposing my entire neck for him to devour. My breasts smash to his hot chest. My hands head south, following the contoured V, acting like an arrow giving me directions. His breath hisses through his teeth as my fingertips slip under his waistband. His reaction encourages me to continue my journey. I grasp his erection. He's hard and heavy in my palm. I'm caught off guard by the velvety-soft skin covering his impressive, rock-hard cock. My free hand tugs one side of his boxers, hoping to unwrap his present for me.

40

TAG

Emma's hand upon my cock, her delicate fingers gently grasping my shaft, fuel my need to bury myself balls deep inside her wet heat. *Slow. How do we go slow? How do I go slow when she pours jet fuel upon my flames of desire? She is young, she is inexperienced, and she was hurt;* I remind myself.

"Tag, I need you inside," she whispers breathily at the same time she tugs.

"Angel," I growl.

"I'm ready," she pleads, breaking through the last of my resolve. She slips her hand from me. Instantly I mourn the loss.

I fall to the bed on her right, removing my boxers with record speed. I reach for a condom, freezing when Emma straddles me. Her bare thighs hug my hips; her hot core presses deliciously to mine. Admiring her bravado, I offer the foil wrapper. Her fingers fumble nervously as they extricate and roll it on. Her tongue clings to the corner of her mouth as she concentrates.

Dressed and ready for action, my cock stands proud. I place my hands upon her hips, feeling the need to ensure she slowly impales herself over me. Her wild eyes on mine, she lowers her entrance to my tip. I am thankful for the desensitizing barrier the condom provides. I will not last long, but I will hold out long enough for Emma to find her release first.

She hinted to her inexperience; I feel I need to guide her even as I let her lead. "Slow," I urge. "Allow yourself to stretch as you go slow. You will find it deeper in this position."

She nods slightly, digs her teeth into her lower lip, and sinks upon me. Her eyes grow wide, and her breath catches. I ab curl to a sitting position, one hand on her hip, the other at her jaw.

"Relax and slow," I encourage, forcing calm into my voice. "Don't hurt yourself. Relax and breathe."

Emma's eyes remain locked to mine. She slowly slides down my shaft. Her hot, wet heat clutches tightly as I slip farther within her. *I need to thrust.* I fight the urge to rut. *I need to claim her.* I fight my primal needs, keeping her safety in the front of my mind.

Barely half way, she takes a deep breath before impaling herself completely. My fingertips bite the flesh of her hips, and my back falls to the mattress. Above me, Emma holds her breath, clenching her teeth.

"Breathe," I remind her through my own clenched teeth.

Her inner walls hold my shaft like a vice grip. I force my fingers to relax, tracing a path up her ribcage. My intention is to help her relax, instead she squirms. I forgot she is ticklish. My movement gives the desired effect. Her jaw relaxes and she draws in breath. She moves her hips infinitesimally, acclimating to my girth.

"I'm okay," she assures me, placing her palms on my abs.

She bites her lip, slowly raising herself. A soft moan escapes as she seats herself once more.

"Tag, I… I'm not sure how to move," she confesses.

"Do what feels good for you," I instruct, reveling in the sensation of her surrounding me.

"I want to do… what you like," she worries.

"Angel, being inside you is already too much for me," I assure her. "Any movement works for me."

Emma

I regret climbing over Tag. *I'm not sure how to...* I push away that train of thought. *I can do this. Move.* I will my thighs to flex, sliding me up then down, up then down. With each movement my body relaxes into the overwhelming sensation of Tag touching the very center of me.

"Help me," I beg.

Tag obliges. His hands at my hips encourage me to grind into him on the downward motion. The groomed smattering of hair of his pubis provides much needed friction on my clit. Over and over, I repeat the motion. Up, down, grind with a moan. Up, down, grind and moan. He moves one hand to pluck my nipples. His gentle tug feels phenomenal. I feel my core winding tighter as my release approaches.

Tag

Sensing her frustration as her orgasm draws near, I place the pad of my thumb to Emma's swollen clit. While she continues climbing up and down my shaft, I press circles into her bundle of nerves. Her head tips back and her chest arches, signaling she's close. On her next downward motion, I thrust myself deep.

"Mm-hmm," she moans, repeating the motion two more times.

"AAHHH!" she screams, body tight, inner walls constricting.

I continue to thrust against her inner contractions. Damn this condom. As amazing as these sensations feel, I imagine bare would be divine. *Thrust. Thrust.*

"Emm..." I moan, emptying myself into the condom, her inner walls milking everything from me.

Emma wilts upon my chest. Her body heaves with her rapid

breathing. Still connected, I rub my fingers along her spine, careful not to tickle her. Her mouth agape upon my shoulder, I feel wet drool dribble from the corner.

"Angel," I croon, pressing my palm flat to her back. "Em… Are you okay?"

It seems silly to ask if she is okay after an orgasm, but as I sought my release, I focused on my need. I seek to ensure I didn't cause her harm.

"Ssss," she slurps, her jaw closing on my shoulder. "Gross, I slobbered on you." She wipes away the moisture with her fingertips. "That's definitely not sexy," she groans.

"That was the best sex of my life," I proclaim. "Feel free to slobber all you want. You've earned it." I quickly deal with the condom.

"Uh-huh," she argues.

I kiss her temple, moving my hands to cup her face. Holding her inches from my face, I reiterate my blissful confession. "You climbing on top was sexy as hell. Everything… All of it… All of you… sex has never felt like that." I detest my inability to vocalize all this experience meant and felt to me. I close my eyes, drawing in a long breath. "I love you," I blurt.

Emma's laser focus burns through me, searching for the truth.

Love? Love. I do…I love her.

Emma winces as she slides off me, crumbling to the mattress. Her hands frantically wrap the sheet around her body. She plans to run. I cannot allow her to flee.

Wrapping my arms around her middle, I spoon her to me. My mouth near her ear, I speak. "It's fast. It's too soon. Hell, everything these past couple of weeks morphed at light speed. I. Love. You."

"It's too much," she whispers. "Overwhelming."

"I've never spoken those three words out loud," I confess. "I've never been in love before. I'm… scared." I hate the emotion heavy in my voice. "The closest thing to love I've ever felt was from Bonnie. I should tell her I love her; I should tell her how much she means to me. You… I don't want to wait to tell you how I feel. I am in love with you, Emma Whatley."

She turns in my arms. When her lips part, I halt her words with my fingers.

"You don't need to say anything. I love you. This is the best sex I've ever experienced, and I needed you to know." I press a long, soft kiss to her forehead.

"What made it the best?" she whispers softly into the darkness.

"You. I am on high alert when you are near. My body gravitates towards you. It's little things… it's everything about you." I trace her lower lip with the pad of my thumb. "You push all my buttons. Something was missing, and now it's not. I've never felt so complete. It's scary. It's not just sexual. My career, my home, my free time—I am happy. You did that. Your challenge to find my niche provided the slap in the face I needed to wake up. I am no longer going through the motions, playing a role in my own life. Emma, I love you."

41

EMMA

Time passes in the blink of an eye. I spend my days recording and posting new recipes or communicating with my followers. My evenings are spent with Tag, Justin, and Rachel. Life after high school is much better than I anticipated.

"Got a minute?" I ask, peeking my head into Tag's office.

He works now with his office door open most days, and gone are the designer suits. Working at home, he now wears business casual attire.

"Always for you," he croons, rising from his seat to greet me.

I wet my lips in anticipation, rising on tip toes to meet his mouth. Even his short, sweet kisses stir emotions within me. I must remind myself that he needs to work, and I came in here with a purpose.

"I have two things to talk to you about," I inform him.

He motions for me to join him on the sofa in the seating area of his office.

"Good news or bad news first?" I ask.

"Good news first," he requests, placing his hands on mine in my lap.

"I did something today," I begin, nervous. "I gave my notice at the restaurant."

Tag's arms envelope me. Tight to his chest, he congratulates me.

"Now for the bad news…" I mutter against his chest.

"I don't want to hear it," he states. "Let's celebrate your career change tonight, and you can share the bad news tomorrow."

I pull my head from his chest. *Avoiding the news will not make it disappear. At least not this time.*

"When was the last time you talked to Justin?" I ask.

Tag's head tilts, and his eyes narrow. "Last night," he answers.

I sigh deeply.

"Pregnant?" he asks and groans at the same time.

I nod.

"Whoa."

Again, I nod.

"I hoped his luck had changed," Tag grumbles. "When are they getting married?"

"Well," I drawl. "I think they are attempting to see this as an exciting new stage of their lives. Instead of an unlucky event. Rachel refuses to get married just because she's pregnant. Apparently, Justin offered to marry her, and she told him to ask her again in a year or two. So…"

"So…" he parrots my word. "Uncle Tag and Aunt Emma need to spoil this little guy starting now."

"Well, I think he is a she," I inform.

"They are having a girl?" Excitement laces his words.

"It's a bit early to know the sex of the baby. Either way…"

Again, Tag interrupts me. "Either way, we get to spoil him or her rotten."

I love his reaction and excitement over their baby. I'd always imagined him as a father. His reaction proves my instincts were spot on. My belly flips, and I bite my lips tight between my teeth.

"Angel," his gravelly voice croons. "What are you thinking?"

I shake my head, not ready to put my happy thoughts into the universe.

Tag leans closer. "I plan to fill our house with little Emma and Tag's one day."

My breath hitches with his words.

"I'm not ready yet," I whisper.

He kisses me, his large hands cupping my face. His forehead to mine, his eyes sear deep within my soul.

"I love you. When we are ready, I will love every minute of creating a family with you," he vows.

42

EMMA

Rachel and I plan to lounge by the pool this afternoon. Waiting for her arrival, I assist Bonnie with lunch. I sauté the onions and peppers while Bonnie flips the chicken breasts out on the grill. My mouth waters with anticipation of the chicken sandwiches we prepare. Fresh lettuce, pickles, sliced tomatoes, and condiments line the island countertop behind me. Bonnie buttered buns that we will grill minutes before we put it all together.

A barking sound echoes through the foyer. I pause my stirring and crane my neck. Unless Bonnie fell upon reentering the house, no one else is home to make any noise. Long quiet seconds pass. Hearing nothing, I begin to stir once again.

Ruff! Ruff!

I freeze.

"Oh lord, what do we have here?" Bonnie chortles.

Ruff! Ruff!

Did a dog get through the fence into our yard? I remove the skillet from the burner, shutting the stove off. Then I walk to investigate.

At the kitchen door, I am greeted by Bing. *How can this be? How did he get here?*

"Surprise!" Tag cheers, arms wide, and a leash dangling from his left hand.

"What...?" I'm dumbstruck.

I kneel, allowing Bing to pepper my cheeks with kisses. Always excited to see me, he seems even more excited to be outside the kennel today.

"Bing and I had a long talk," Tag claims, smiling proudly. "He agreed to be a good boy if I agreed to become a dog lover."

His trademark, dazzling smile on display, his green eyes convey his worry of my reaction to this gesture. It does not escape me that this is a grand gesture, requiring sacrifice on his part. My hand over my heart, I battle the tears welling in my eyes.

"You adopted him?" My voice squeaks.

Tag bends down, and Bing rolls onto his back. Displaying his belly, Tag wastes no time awarding him with the rubs he desires.

"We grew on each other," Tag explains. "This house and yard are plenty big enough for one more resident."

I tilt my head to one side, eyes on his. *He did this for me.* In his efforts to spend more time with me, he learned all about my affection for the dogs at the ARL. *He brought Bing home for me.*

Tag

I take Emma's inability to talk and tears as a sign she likes my gift. I long to buy her many things, and she refuses every one. I knew she would not return this gift from me. My heart warms at her happiness. *I gave her this. I plan to give her many more gifts to bring her joy.*

"Bing, let's go outside," I urge, walking toward the patio doors with him on my heels.

I bend down to unhook his leash before he darts to explore in the fenced in yard. I feel Emma's presence beside me as I keep a watchful eye on Bing. *Perhaps I should have asked Barry to inspect the fence for any possible holes for a dog to escape. I hope he does not hop into the pool.*

"I can't believe you did this for me," she whispers.

"I didn't do it for you," I correct. "I did it for us. I've never had a pet. I am twenty-three-years-old and decided it was about time I took responsibility and opened my heart to a furry friend."

"So, this isn't a gift for me?" she teases, acting offended.

"He can be a gift for both of us," I state.

"Bing, go potty!" Emma orders.

Instantly, he freezes, his attention on her for a moment. He takes three more steps before lifting his right, hind leg and hosing down a fence post.

"He may kill your grass," she giggles.

I shrug. "If he does, Barry will have more to keep him busy this summer," I answer.

I surprise even myself that brown spots in the grass seem frivolous to me now. A month ago, I would be on a tirade at the thought of a person or animal tainting my perfect green grass.

Bing returns and sits on the patio at my right, looking up to me expectantly.

"I suppose you think you earned another treat," I laugh.

"Another?" Emma inquires. "You bought him treats?"

I nod, signaling for Bing to follow us into the house. "Bonnie bought them on her last trip to the grocery store. I wanted to be prepared for picking him up today."

Emma's brow furrows at the realization that this was not a spur of the moment idea today. Now she knows I discussed this with Bonnie and planned prior to adopting Bing. I thought of Bing and Emma's love for him daily since my visit to the ARL. I got the idea while there. When I came home, I looked at the house as a pet owner for any dangers or changes that might need to be made. I weighed the pros and cons of adopting him, discussed the idea with Bonnie, and planned for his arrival before driving there this morning.

"Where should we set up his kennel, bed, toy box, and food

dish?" I ask Emma, catching her off guard once more. "I can't take the credit. I asked Bonnie and Barry to ensure we had everything we might need for his arrival."

Emma's eyes and smile dazzle me. She bounces as she walks, leading the way. *I did this; I made her this happy.*

43

TAG

Standing at my office window, I see Emma's silhouette move about the kitchen of the pool house. In the months since her eighteenth birthday, my life flipped one-hundred-eighty degrees for the better. The swim pool between our two workspaces sees us swimming much fewer laps of frustration and enjoying more hours lounging by the pool with our friends.

I love using my wealth to make dreams of fellow Iowans become a reality. With each diverse investment, I learn a wealth of information in a new field. Emma's keen observation and challenge proved to be the key to finding happiness and fulfillment in my career.

With Emma by my side, I sleep better at night. Gone are my late night swims full of contemplation. Mr. Sandman and I are no longer enemies. I feel better about myself, the avenues in which I earn money, and my spending habits. I no longer pretend that shiny, expensive items bring me joy. No, I didn't move out of the mansion or donate my vehicles. Instead, I take pride in investing to help others achieve their dreams, volunteer to better our community, and enjoy the simple moments with family and friends. With Emma's help, I learned to take pride in the life I lead, the work I do, and the relationships I nurture.

Speaking of relationships, I am head over heels in love with an amazing woman. I love everything about her, even her quirks. I am no longer embarrassed by the variety of seasonings she carries in her purse. I love that sometimes she takes it upon herself to share them with nearby patrons at restaurants. She continues to encourage me to try new things in every aspect of my life. Some might say our lives are perfect. While they are amazing, we do still face challenges.

EPILOGUE

EMMA

I pull my vibrating cell phone from my pocket.

TAG

dinner in 10

"Weird," I mumble.

"What's weird?" Rachel asks, as she fastens a fresh diaper on her daughter.

"Mimi," Tiffany points in my direction with the fingers of the hand not in her mouth.

At one and a half, she is a drooling, teething machine.

"Tag texted that dinner is in ten minutes," I inform her with a scowl. "I guess I need to go."

"I bet the surprise he created in the pool house is ready. Don't forget to send me pics. I'm anxious to see what he installed for you this time." She smiles at me as she lowers Tiffany to the floor of the nursery.

I pepper kisses on the plump cheeks of the cutest toddler in the world before I make the quick drive home. With Rachel and Justin still living in the pool house of his parent's place, it's a short golf cart ride for me to get my baby fix.

Tag's secretive announcement this morning in kicking me out of my own workspace tortured my thoughts all afternoon. I assume it's an early birthday present. I don't really need anything for my blog, so I have no idea what he might be up to.

Tag

The kitchen timer beeps, and my nerves skyrocket. Dinner will be ready in ten minutes. I fight the urge to peek at my short ribs. Why I chose a protein that cooks for three hours as my first solo meal confounds me. With the time I spend next to Emma in her kitchen, I felt like Superman when I chose to prepare braised short ribs for her.

If I am being honest, the meal is not the cause of my nerves. It is the little blue box in my left pants pocket. No, I did not spend an exurbanite amount on the perfect engagement ring at Tiffany's. We both know Emma would detest the thought of it. Like the woman I plan to propose to this evening, I hunted for a simple, yet stunning setting.

Rachel, Justin, and I visited many second-hand and jewelry stores scattered throughout the state. I appraised engagement rings everywhere I went. That is why I approached first Kate and then Barry for their assistance. Together we designed a new custom ring for Bonnie, combining Bonnie's mom's and grandmother's wedding rings, and she donated one of her stones for Emma's ring. The simple ring in my pocket contains a stone from Bonnie's family's rings. I am proud to present it to Emma, and I know she will absolutely love it.

Well, she will love it once she throws a fit for the Tiffany's box I placed it in. She will only be mad for a moment. When I tell her that Justin plans to present the true Tiffany's ring in this box to Rachel tomorrow night, she will forgive me for the small prank.

The End

Enjoy other *7 Deadly Sins Series of stand-alone books* available now.

The final story in the series:

Unhinged, 7 Deadly Sins: Wrath releases in **2023**.

Help other readers find this book and give me a giant author hug—
please consider leaving a review on Amazon, Goodreads, and
BookBub

a few words mean so much.

Check out my **Pinterest Boards** for my inspirations
for characters, settings, and recipes.
(Link on the following pages.)

ALSO BY HALEY RHOADES:

Trivia Page

1. Character names in this book are those of the characters of the sitcom *Friends* and *Seinfeld*. (Except the ARL volunteer, Dawn)

2. The character Dawn is based on my best friend. During a car ride, I explained my next series of books and she suggested I have one random character that appears in each book. Thus, I named the character after her and awarded her Dawn's positive spirit. In 2015 she was diagnosed with stage IV colon cancer. They found it late and it had spread throughout her body. She had chemotherapy every two weeks for all 8 years of her cancer battle. With all of this she was still a ray of sunshine and lifted others, like me, up. Her strength and selflessness inspire me to try and improve myself. She was the most upbeat and positive woman I know. I absolutely loved her laugh. She lost her battle with colon cancer in February 2023.

3. What are the seven deadly sins? The 7 deadly sins, also called 7 cardinal sins, are transgressions that are fatal to spiritual progress within Christian teachings. They include envy, gluttony, greed, anger or wrath, sloth, and pride. They are the converse of the 7 heavenly virtues.

4. My pen name is a combination of 2 of my paternal great-grandmothers' maiden names. (Haley and Rhoades)

ABOUT THE AUTHOR

Haley Rhoades's writing is another bucket-list item coming to fruition, just like meeting Stephen Tyler, Ozzie Smith, and skydiving. As she continues to write contemporary romance, she also writes sweet romance and young adult books under the name Brooklyn Bailey, as well as children's books under the name Gretchen Stephens. She plans to complete her remaining bucket-list items, including ghost-hunting, storm-chasing, and bungee jumping. She is a Netflix-binging, Converse-wearing, avidly-reading, traveling geek.

A team player, Haley thrived as her spouse's career moved the family of four, thirteen times to three states. One move occurred eleven days after a C-section. Now with two adult sons, Haley copes with her newly emptied nest by writing and spoiling Nala, her Pomsky. A fly on the wall might laugh as she talks aloud to her fur-baby all day long.

Haley's under five-foot, fun-size stature houses a full-size attitude. Her uber-competitiveness in all things entertains, frustrates, and challenges family and friends. Not one to shy away from a dare, she faces the consequences of a lost bet no matter the humiliation. Her fierce loyalty extends from family, to friends, to sports teams.

Haley's guilty pleasures are Lifetime and Hallmark movies. Her other loves include all things peanut butter, *Star Wars*, mathematics, and travel. Past day jobs vary tremendously from an elementary special-education para-professional, to a YMCA sports director, to a retail store accounting department, and finally a high school mathematics teacher.

Haley resides with her husband and fur-baby in the Des Moines area. This Missouri-born girl enjoys the diversity the Midwest offers.

Reach out on Facebook, Twitter, Instagram, or her website…she would love to connect with her readers.

Social Media & Author Websites:
https://linktr.ee/haleyrhoades
http://www.haleyrhoades.com/

amazon.com/author/haleyrhoades

goodreads.com/haleyrhoadesauthor

bookbub.com/authors/haley-rhoades

tiktok.com/@haleyrhoadesauthor

instagram.com/haleyrhoadesauthor

facebook.com/AuthorHaleyRhoades

twitter.com/HaleyRhoadesBks

youtube.com/@haleyrhoadesbrooklynbaileyauth

pinterest.com/haleyrhoadesaut

patreon.com/ginghamfrog

linkedin.com/in/haleyrhoadesauthor

Made in the USA
Monee, IL
25 April 2023

32404051R00125